Sammy-Jo Hopkins

# feather Wars

# feather Wars

## Sally Grindley

**BLOOMSBURY**

My thanks go to The Royal Pigeon Racing Association in Cheltenham, who provided me with important background information on a subject about which I knew nothing, and to Mrs Pat Humphries whose husband kept pigeons during the war and who was able to give me a fuller understanding of their role. Thanks too, to 'Whitey' for putting me right on several points that didn't make sense to a non-pigeon-keeping writer.

First published in Great Britain in 2003
Bloomsbury Publishing Plc, 38 Soho Square, London W1D 3HB

A CIP catalogue record for this book is available from the British Library

ISBN 0 7475 6338 1

Printed in Great Britain by Clays Ltd, St Ives plc

10 9 8 7 6 5 4 3 2 1

*For Chris Atwell*
*I did it Chris, I only wish you were here to read it*

# CHAPTER ONE

Matt stood in the open doorway and saluted. Sam looked at him shyly. His brother looked older in his uniform, and somehow rather important.

'See you at Easter,' said Matt.

'Wish I could go too.'

'They don't take kids in nappies where I'm going,' grinned Matt. He aimed a playful punch at Sam's chin. Sam thumped him in the stomach.

'Don't hit Matty,' cried Clare. She pushed Sam out of the way and threw herself into Matt's arms. Matt tossed her high in the air, then hugged her tight and ruffled her dark brown curls.

'Bye bye, my little chocolatey Clare. Be good for Mummy and I'll bring you back a stick of rock.' He lowered her to the floor and put his arms round his mother.

'Look after yourself, Matthew,' said Hetty Lonsdale. 'Write to us with news whenever you can. We'll be thinking of you.'

'Chin up, Mum,' said Matt cheerfully. 'I'll be back before you know it.' He kissed her on the cheek, and moved forward to shake hands with his father. Arthur Lonsdale was having none of that. He grasped his eldest child by the shoulders and held him tight.

'Take care, son,' he whispered. In that moment, Sam was shocked to see that his father was close to tears.

Matt broke away hurriedly and picked up his bags. 'Got to go,' he said. 'Can't keep Blighty waiting.'

He heaved his backpack up over his shoulders, pushed his way through the door, but turned round again. 'Don't let the midges bite,' he whispered to Sam, then he strode down the path, out through the gate, and marched off along the road towards the village.

Sam stood in the doorway and watched his brother's back until it disappeared round a corner. Then he closed the door and ran upstairs to his bedroom, his and Matt's bedroom, except that Matt wasn't there to share it any more. The spaces left by the few things that Matt had taken with him seemed like great black holes, yet the crumpled sheets of his unmade bed appeared to mock with their attempt to pretend that everything was normal; that their occupier would be back that night.

Sam turned away and gazed out of the bedroom window. Below, his father was walking down the long garden path, carrying a bowl full of corn. Sam watched as he reached the wooden building at the end of the path and went inside, then he kicked his bedroom wall, shouted, 'Stupid pigeons! Stupid, stupid pigeons!' and threw himself on to his bed.

Clare came into the room sucking her thumb and clasping a shabby rag doll.

'Mummy says it's your turn to lay the table,' she said, triumphantly, 'and you're to do it now.'

'Go away,' shouted Sam, 'and take that rotten, smelly doll with you.'

Clare burst into tears. 'I hate you, Samuel Lonsdale,' she cried, 'and I wish you'd gone away and not Matty, and I'm going to tell Mummy of you.'

'Tell-tale-tit,' retorted Sam as she fled, but he felt rather ashamed. It wasn't Clare's fault that there was a war on, that his brother had gone away to fight, that he dreaded going back to school now that the Christmas holidays were over, that he felt so useless, that his father was too wrapped up in his pigeons to care. But that wasn't fair either, was it? Hadn't he just seen for himself that his father cared, even though most of the time he tried not to show it? Or was it that when he tried to show it, Sam pushed him away? He went to the window again and made an effort to cheer himself up with an image of his father wrapped up in pigeons. 'Funny language, English,' he mused.

His mother knocked on the door and came in. 'Why so angry, Sam?' she asked gently. 'We're all hurting, even Clare. Particularly Clare, perhaps, because she doesn't understand what's happening, except that someone she loves has gone away.'

Sam shifted uncomfortably. A voice inside him protested that he had the right to hurt the most, but he found himself saying, 'Why are we carrying on as though nothing's happened? I mean, like taking turns at laying the table, going back to school, feeding pigeons, scrubbing behind our ears even? What's the point?'

'Because,' said his mother, 'if we stop, then we will become paralysed with fear and sadness. And if we put our heads in our hands and weep, then we will be betraying Matthew and all the other brave men who have gone to fight on our behalf. We owe it to them to try to keep going, so that when they come home there is something for them to come home to. End of speech. Now, are you going to lay that table, or am I going to wallop you with the dish mop?'

'Wallop me with the dish mop,' grinned Sam, 'but first you've got to catch me!' He darted past her, flew downstairs into the kitchen, picked up the dish mop himself, wet it, and stood ready to attack. As soon as his mother came into the kitchen, he smacked the dish mop round her neck and headed off down the garden path, hysterical with laughter. Hetty raced after him, Clare trotted after them both, determined to join in the fun. They fell down on the grass in a giggling heap, just as Arthur Lonsdale came out of the pigeon loft. In his hands, he held a dead pigeon.

'I should have noticed before,' he said, 'but with everything else going on ... They just pecked away at it, until it gave up. I should have noticed it wasn't strong enough to fight back.'

'Poor little pigeon,' said Clare. 'Will it go to heaven?'

'I'm sure it will,' said Hetty.

Sam wondered why the fuss about one pigeon when there were dozens more in the pigeon-loft: dozens more all the same, all noisy, all messy, all taking up too much of his father's time, and now spoiling the bit of fun they were having in the middle of an unhappy day. Worse than that – but no, no, no, he wasn't going to think about it. He refused to think about it.

Supper was a gloomy affair that evening, despite Hetty's attempts to cheer everyone up. The blackout curtains didn't help. Not a glimmer of lamplight could leak out, but neither could a glimmer of moonlight trickle in. Arthur hardly spoke. Clare babbled anxiously about starting school and could she take her doll and how would she know where to go and what if nobody liked her and what if a bomb fell.

Sam realised with a pang just how much they were going to miss Matt. Matt had such an easy way about him; everyone relaxed in his company, even his father. He wasn't especially good-looking or clever, but he drew people to him with his big smile and the way he grabbed life with both hands and took out of it what he wanted.

'Lucky army,' thought Sam. 'They'd better send him back.' Then, as the forbidden fears began to crowd in again, Sam thought, 'Stupid army, stupid Hitler, stupid war! It's your fault Matt won't be there tomorrow.'

Sam struggled to get to sleep that night. It was strange not having his brother snuffling and grunting beside him. His mother had stripped Matt's bed and left only the eiderdown over the mattress. No pretence of normality there any more. Matt had gone away, and Sam had no doubt that tomorrow he would have to face the consequences of his brother's absence.

When at last Sam fell asleep, he dreamed that the spaces left by the things Matt had taken grew and grew until they formed one enormous black hole, which swallowed him up. There was no way out of the hole, but pigeons found their way in and began to peck at him, over and over again. He hit out at them with his fists and feet, but they kept coming at him. He curled himself into a tight ball, but still they pecked at him, until just as he was about to give up, he woke. He lay there, motionless, in the pitch dark, terrified that the pigeons were in his room. He felt around for the torch on his bedside table and switched it on, comforted by the beam of light. When he felt safe again, he jumped out of bed and moved some of his own things into the gaps left by Matt.

He woke up next morning exhausted, and knew that the nightmare might now begin for real.

# CHAPTER TWO

Nothing happened. All day long Sam waited, but nothing. Perhaps they hadn't realised that Matt wasn't around, that Matt had gone away. Perhaps they hadn't had the opportunity. Perhaps they were just bored with the whole tiresome thing. For that's what it was, Sam could see that, when he wasn't being eaten away by it. Tiresome, annoying, tedious, hardly the stuff of nightmares. Yet, the relentlessness of it made it nightmarish.

But today, nothing. Sam had walked slowly along the country roads close to home. He was safe enough there and had waved his mother and Clare on as they overtook him on their bicycles, on their way to Clare's new school. He could have gone with them on his own bike, the infant school was close to his own, but that might have made things worse, and he didn't want Clare involved.

It was a cold, bleak mid-January morning. The sky was still hung over from the night before and threatened to smother a faint tinge of pink creeping up from the horizon. Most of the fields were ploughed bare, the heavy brown soil forbidding the slightest hint that new life was stirring underneath. Where the land was laid to grass, sheep huddled together for warmth. 'No one would guess there is a war on, and that soon there might be fighting here,' thought Sam.

When he had reached the main street leading into the village, he had felt like turning back, but had forced himself on. The churchyard was a favourite hiding-place, and the alley by the baker's, the first World War Memorial, the corner by the garage. Sam walked quickly past them all, steeling himself against the expected assault, but it hadn't come. He turned into the school playground with a sigh of relief and lost himself amongst his friends. So far so good.

They were there, of course. Sam never doubted

they would be. He saw them across the playground even as he swopped Christmas holiday news with his friends, but if they saw him they showed no sign. At least he was able to relax when he was in the classroom: they were in the year above him. At breaktime and lunchtime he made sure that he was never on his own, and each time he returned to the classroom he checked his desk and satchel. When he passed through the school gates at the end of that first day, he saw them going off in the opposite direction. Just as he had kept out of their way, they had kept out of his.

As the week went on and still nothing happened, Sam grew more confident. Perhaps Matt's warnings had frightened them off for good. He quickly found himself caught up in the constant bombilation of excitement that gripped the school. Dozens of evacuees had been billeted in the village and were joining in with classes. Most of them came from big towns or cities, and they met with a barrage of questions about what was happening there, and had there been any bombs, and did they have cars, and how long were they staying. For their part, the evacuees

17

wanted to know what they should do if they met a poacher, and were the apples on the trees edible, and was it true that people drank milk straight from a cow, and how would they know when it was safe to go home. Sam was fascinated by their different accents, and intrigued by how seemingly streetwise yet how ignorant some of them were, especially the Londoners. They added a welcome dash of exotic to the normally drab school routine. Moreover, the talk of war and blackouts, and the lessons on air-raid procedures and aircraft identification, lent a general air of anticipation to each day that helped to dull Sam's own private anxieties.

But then, on Friday, it began. Sam was on his way home from school, walking along the main street out of the village, when he saw them ahead of him, on the other side of the road, sitting on the church wall. They looked round and saw him, then carried on talking.

Sam tried to keep calm as a shiver of fear shot down his spine. 'Just ignore them,' he said to himself. 'They can't do any harm.' He stared straight ahead, kept on walking, and pretended he hadn't noticed them. They allowed him to go a few yards past them, without appearing to be interested in him, then stood up and began to follow him, still on the other side of the road.

Sam's heart began to pound. He quickened his pace. He was almost jogging, when he heard, 'Cooee! Coo-coo-coo-ee! What's the hu-rree?' Then they turned round and sauntered off, sniggering, in the opposite direction. That was it. Nothing more. Just enough to let Sam know that he hadn't escaped.

# CHAPTER THREE

Feathers across his face, over his nose – 'Can't breathe, can't breathe!' Peck, peck, peck. 'Go away. Leave me alone!' Sam sat bolt upright in bed.

'Time to get up, lazybones,' said Clare, jumping to the floor. 'Your breakfast is getting cold and it's bacon and Mummy says it might be the last bit of bacon we have for a while because of rashering.'

With the blackout across his window, Sam wouldn't have known whether it was the middle of the night or the middle of the day, if it weren't for Clare furiously tickling his face with a feather, insisting that he get up 'now!', and the smell of breakfast assaulting his senses. 'Rationing,' he corrected her, smiling in spite of himself.

He crawled out of bed, opened the curtains and

looked out. It was a cold, bright, breezy, January morning, the thinnest wisps of cloud scuttering across an otherwise flawless blue sky. His father was just on his way indoors, leaving behind him a freshly dug square of earth where previously there had been lawn. Sam shivered, scrambled into his clothes and ran downstairs.

'Good evening,' said Arthur Lonsdale, without looking up from washing his hands.

'Good morning,' replied Sam. 'Nice day, isn't it?'

'Wonderful,' said Arthur. 'What a pity you missed it!'

'I'd better have tomorrow's breakfast now, then, in case I miss tomorrow,' chuckled Sam, sitting down quickly.

'Breakfast for the workers,' said his mother, carrying in plates of bacon, eggs, beans and toast.

'I'm a worker, aren't I, Daddy?' piped up Clare, her round cheeks pinched pink by the cold. 'I've been helping Daddy clean out the pigeons, so I can have lots of breakfast.'

'Big deal.' Sam tucked into his breakfast. This was the weekend, and the weekend was his refuge. He wasn't going to panic every time pigeons were mentioned. 'Why are you digging up the garden, Dad?'

'We need to grow our own vegetables. If this war goes on for any length of time, there'll be shortages of most things.'

'It won't though, will it?'

'Who knows, son? Best be prepared for anything though, eh?'

Sam nodded his head. 'Best be prepared for anything,' he mused.

After breakfast, Sam wandered down the garden. His father had gone back to his digging. Sam peered into the pigeon-loft. There must have been nearly thirty birds inside. Some were feeding, some were preening, others were cooing gently. They all looked the same to Sam, but his father had a name for each one, knew how old they were, and whether or not they were ready for racing.

'When's the next race?' he asked, not that he really cared.

'There's never any racing in the winter, Sam, you must know that. And there'll be no more racing now anyway till the war's over.'

Sam was surprised. 'Why not?'

'The birds might fall into enemy hands and be used for spying.'

An image of a pigeon hiding in a cupboard and secretly spying on someone flashed into Sam's mind and he began to giggle. But his father continued: 'Of course, if we're invaded then I'll have to destroy the whole lot of them. Now, are you going to stand there all day chatting, or are you going to help me with this digging? There's snow forecast and the ground will be too hard if I leave it much longer.'

Sam picked up a fork and turned the ground over in silence. Destroy the whole lot of them? He was shocked at the thought of what his father might have to do, of the pain that it would cause him. What would Matt have said now if he had been here? Sam was sure that he would have been able to cheer his father up and convince him that there would be no invasion. But what did he, Sam, know? How could a twelve-year-old speak with any persuasion about the likely course of world affairs? His parents, he knew, tried to protect him from 'worst scenario' discussions. His father's reference to one awful consequence of invasion had been a slip-up, but it hung over them now like an executioner's blade.

Sam was relieved when his father lay down his spade and said, 'I'm going to fetch the potato tubers from town. Do you want to come with me, Sam?'

'You bet!'

'Put some warmer clothes on, then. It'll be freezing on the old banger.'

This was a rare treat. If Matt had been there, he would have gone. Sam had often envied him the time he spent with his father. Now it was his turn. He rushed into the house and pulled on his duffel coat, woollen scarf and gloves, ignoring Clare's demands to know where he was going, and grabbing one of the scones Hetty had just removed from the oven.

'Make sure you hold on tight,' said Arthur as he pushed his motorcycle away from the side of the house, rolled it down the path and out through the gate. Sam clambered on to the back and wrapped his arms round his father's waist. He enjoyed the feeling of safety it gave him, and when the engine spluttered into life he leaned his face against his father's back.

It was ten miles to the nearest town. On the way

they passed through several small villages and hamlets, where people waved them down and asked if Arthur had much work what with the war, and was Hetty well, and had the little one started school, and my what a big lad Sam was, and were they missing Matthew yet. Sam was secretly pleased at how popular his father seemed to be, though he was keen to get going again and wished people wouldn't keep ruffling his hair. His father, Sam noticed, avoided becoming involved in any village gossip, but said just enough about his own affairs not to appear impolite. And from what he said, Sam gathered that all might not be well. His work as a master carpenter was drying up under the threat of invasion.

The streets of the town were packed despite the cold. The weekly market in the square regularly drew crowds from outlying villages, and now that some articles and foodstuffs were growing scarce in the local village shops, and with warnings of heavy snow to come, the market was busier than ever. Sam was entranced by the colour and the bustle and the noise. Brightly patterned awnings round the stalls flapped merrily in the breeze. Stallholders stamped their feet and clapped their hands to keep themselves warm, while they shouted themselves hoarse to encourage people to buy. Customers moved from one stall to the next, picking things up and putting them down again, haggling over prices and complaining about shortages.

Arthur made his way to a stall where all sorts of garden tools, plants, bulbs, seed packets and animal foods were spread out in neat rows. He chatted animatedly to the stallholder, who clearly knew him well, about planting times, soil types and the best fertilisers, and gave Sam a large bag of potato tubers to hold while he picked out a variety of packets of vegetable seeds. He then pulled a hessian bag from his rucksack and asked for several pounds of corn for his pigeons.

'They'll be rationing this if the war comes,' the stallholder warned. 'The price is already going up, along with everything else.'

Just as the stallholder poured the corn on to the scales, Sam saw one of them. He was standing with his back to the stall opposite, and gazing directly at Sam, his father and their tell-tale purchase. Sam felt waves of panic well up inside. Suddenly, he wanted to put as much distance as he could between his father and himself, anything to make it look as though they were not together. But it was too late, and he knew it. Caught red-handed. Guilty, guilty, guilty. He turned away, but not before he had seen the boy smirk and wink at him. When Sam looked round again, he was sauntering off with his mother.

'All right, Sam?' Arthur was pushing the bag of corn into his rucksack. 'You look as though you've seen a ghost.'

'Can we go home now?' muttered Sam. Another day ruined. Another weekend ruined.

'I thought we might have a cup of tea and some cake before we go back. Wouldn't you like that?'

Sam shook his head adamantly, not trusting himself to speak, and began to walk quickly away. He didn't want his father to be nice to him, didn't want to be near him, because, at that moment, he hated him.

# CHAPTER FOUR

Every day of the following week was a torment. Time and again, Sam recalled the troubled look on his father's face as he tried to understand where the barrier kept coming from that estranged him from his son. But however much a part of Sam wanted things to be all right between them, he couldn't forget the falsely conspiratorial wink the boy had given him, knowing that it signalled more trouble to come.

It didn't come straight away. This was their new game, was it? Let Sam think he's safe, then hit him just when he begins to relax. Except that Sam didn't relax, not for one moment. He knew he hadn't been let off the hook, knew they were just reeling out the line, letting him think he had escaped. That's what made it worse. How can you stop something when nothing is actually happening? Even if he had wanted to, he couldn't have told anyone. What was there to tell? A coo-coo-cooee and a wink? That would stand up in court, wouldn't it? What about the months before Matt had intervened, then? Well, that had been dealt with, hadn't it? Just ignore them, Sam, and stop tormenting yourself. Voices of despair, voices of reason, voices of naivety, all talking to each other, across each other, round and round in circles, shouting each other down, solving nothing.

The new game. A waiting game. Monday, Tuesday, Wednesday, Thursday, all passed by without the slightest indication that the boy and his cronies were even aware of Sam's existence. So it was to be Friday again, was it? 'Best be prepared, then,' Sam echoed his father's words. 'Expect the worst.'

On Friday morning, Sam woke and lay still for a moment trying to orientate himself. What time was it? He could hear voices below, but no one had come to drag him out of bed. He pulled the blankets right up round his neck. He wasn't going to get up before he had to, and besides it was freezing. He closed his eyes and waited. No one came. Surely it wasn't that early?

Unable to contain his curiosity any longer, Sam sat up in bed, braced himself, then plunged across the room and opened the blackout. The brightness stung him blind for a brief second: everywhere was sparkling white. Snow had buried the garden, to a depth of two feet in places, and was still drifting down like puffs of candyfloss, which hovered and danced before coming to rest. The weaker branches of the trees drooped wearily under their icy topping. A blackbird landing near the end of one of the branches caused a mini avalanche as it bobbed up and down. At the bottom of the garden, the pigeon-loft had taken on the guise of a huge Christmas cake, its roof and sides moulded with thick icing, its windows tiny, like pressed-on chocolate buttons.

As Sam took in this new white world, his father pushed open the back door and began to make his way slowly across the garden in his wellington boots. Sam chuckled because he looked so funny. Arthur had to pull each leg up out of the snow and lift it as high as he could before putting it down in front of the other one. Behind him, a row of oval holes opened up one by one, joined together by a trail of scuffed snow. When at last he reached the shed, Arthur knocked the snow away from the door, making great outward sweeps with his arms, and Sam laughed again at such mole-like shovelling.

Snow. Lots of snow. What about school? No school! Sam leapt into his dressing-gown and charged downstairs.

'It's been snowing, Mum. It's really deep. Does that mean we can't go to school?'

Hetty looked up from kneading a lump of dough. 'I know this will come as a great disappointment to you, Sam, but, no, I'm afraid you won't be able to go to school today. The roads haven't been cleared so we're cut off.'

'What a shame! And I was so looking forward to my lessons.'

Sam pouted, then made a grab for a piece of cake that was lying on the side. Hetty was quicker and smacked him on the back of the hand with a wooden spoon, sending Clare into howls of laughter.

'Serves you right, serves you right!' she chanted. 'Mummy said I can have that piece of cake because I've been helping her.'

'Ooooh, little Miss Goody-Goody.'

'Stop it, you two. Now, Sam, I want you to have your breakfast, then go and help your father clear the path down to the loft.'

'Do I have to? It's too cold.'

'Well then, when you've finished the path you can bring in some wood and lay the fire.'

Hetty had an answer for everything, and Sam knew there was no point in arguing. Besides, anything was better than going to school.

He dressed then went outside to find that his father had already cleared the snow from round the back door and was stripped down to his shirtsleeves, his face beaming red from exertion. Arthur stopped work and leaned on his shovel.

'Bet I can throw a snowball further than you,' he challenged.

'Ha!' laughed Sam. 'Bet you can't.'

'We'll soon see about that.'

Arthur bent over, quickly kneading some snow into a ball, and Sam followed suit.

'After three,' said Arthur. 'One, two, three.'

They hurled their snowballs as hard as they could.

Sam's landed plum in the centre of the pigeon-loft roof. His father's sailed on over the back fence.

'You'll frighten my pigeons,' Arthur teased. 'They'll think a bomb's landed on their roof.'

'Pigeons can't think, Dad,' mocked Sam. 'They're birdbrains.'

'Don't you insult my feathered friends.'

Arthur picked up a snowball and threw it at Sam's chest. Sam was quick to retaliate and caught his father on the bottom as be bent down to fashion a new missile.

'Bulls-eye!' he yelled.

Arthur responded with a shot to the back of the neck which slid icily down inside Sam's jumper.

'Take that!' he whooped.

Sam opened up with a large snowball that bounced off the top of Arthur's head – 'The winner!' – just as Clare came stumbling into the garden.

'Don't hit my Daddy,' she cried, grabbing hold of Arthur's hand and hugging him protectively.

Sam made another snowball and hurled it with all his might at his sister's back. It missed and caught her on the side of the face. Clare screamed and burst into tears.

'Be careful, Sam,' his father remonstrated.

'I didn't mean to,' shouted Sam. 'Anyway, why does she always have to spoil things?'

Arthur was too busy ministering to Clare to pay him any further attention. Sam stormed up to his bedroom and hoped that his father would come and find him, but he soon heard him return to his shovelling, while Clare chattered away as though nothing had happened.

Sam stood by the window and watched for a few minutes, until he saw his mother go out with some food for the birds and stay to help clear the path. He flew down the stairs, out through the back door and almost snatched the spade from Hetty.

'I'm doing that,' he said fiercely, 'and then I'm going to help Clare build a snowman.'

Hetty gaped at Sam, then shrugged her shoulders in bemusement, while Clare skipped around singing, 'A snowman, a snowman, we're going to build a snowman.'

Sam stared across the garden for some reaction from his father, but the minute Arthur looked his way he plunged his spade into the ground and began to dig furiously.

Sam quarried away at the snow until he was dropping with exhaustion, but still he kept going.

'You'll make a hole in the path if you're not careful!' Arthur laughed.

Sam didn't smile, just carried on digging.

When the path was clear all the way to the loft, he went to the wood pile and began to carry logs into the front room, ready to lay a fire. Arthur followed him indoors and stood behind him as he broke some sticks on to the pieces of screwed-up paper on the hearth.

'I don't know what I'm supposed to have done,' Arthur said at last, 'but can we call a truce, please? Or would you like an effigy of me to burn on your fire?'

Sam carried on fiddling with the sticks.

'I'd like to be friends, Sam, but you keep pushing me away and I don't understand why. Can't we talk?'

Sam lit a match and held it to the paper in the hearth. He watched the flame begin to lick at the paper, and the edges of the paper begin to crumple, before it burst into flames which wrapped themselves around the broken sticks and caused them to hiss and spit. And, as he watched, the moment when he might have made an effort to heal the wound that festered untended between himself and his father passed him by. Arthur went back outside, and Sam was snatched from his mute self-absorption when a carrot was thrust in front of his nose.

'I got this for our snowman, Sammy.' Clare waved the carrot excitedly. 'And Mummy says we can have two big black buttons for his eyes and an old scarf and Daddy's old cap. So come on, Sammy, I want to make him now.'

Sam allowed himself to be pulled out into the garden and began to build a mound of snow just by the back door. As he worked and Clare danced around throwing snow in the air and adding the odd handful to the heap that would become the snowman's body, Sam's mood softened. He gazed over to where his father was clearing snow from the front of the pigeon-loft and waited for him to look up. When he did so, his father smiled, but it was a sad smile and Sam knew that at that time there was nothing he could do about it.

# CHAPTER FIVE

By Monday the roads had been cleared and it was possible for Sam to go back to school, even though it was still snowing intermittently and snow was banked up along the sides of the roads, above head height in places. The biting cold forbade any possibility of a thaw, and the sky hung dark and morose.

Walking in the gloom, the noise of his boots on the frozen tarmac echoing all around, Sam could fancy himself the only person on earth, the sole survivor of a major catastrophe, or a hero on his way to fight a terrifying monster, with unseen dangers lurking round every corner. He broke a small branch from a tree and brandished it savagely as he dawdled along, his trusty sword for defeating his enemies.

When he reached the edge of the village, Sam

threw down the branch and trod warily along the icy pavements. Suddenly, he heard footsteps behind him, and he was no longer the only person on earth. He looked round. It was them. He began to walk faster, but in his haste he slipped and landed unceremoniously on his bottom.

He tried to stand up, but his feet kept slithering away from underneath him. And then they walked past him, in single file, staring straight ahead.

Sam sat on the ground waiting for them to turn round, for the taunts to begin. He braced himself. His heart was thumping in protest, but if they were going to attack him, he was determined to fight back.

'Sticks and stones,' he said to himself. They carried on walking. 'Come on then, what are you waiting for? You've got me where you want me.' Still they carried on walking, until they were out of sight beyond the garage.

Sam heaved himself to his feet, anger knotting his stomach even more than it would have done had they actually said something.

That afternoon, on the way home in the

continuing gloom, the same thing happened. Sam had set off from school immediately the bell sounded, hoping to give them no time to prepare an ambush ahead of him. But they overtook him as he passed the alleyway, in single file again and appearing to ignore him. They must have seen him dash out of school, must have walked as fast as they could to catch him up. He waited again for them to turn round, but they didn't. They reached the church and strolled off down the side street that led to the river.

Once he had left the village, Sam sat on a gate at the edge of a field and tried to calm himself down.

'Don't get so wound up about things,' he heard Matt saying. 'You're like a coiled spring waiting to snap.'

But it was the not knowing when they would strike, how far they would go, where it would all end, that was gnawing at him now.

The image of his father's dead pigeon came back to him. The other birds had pecked away at it, gradually weakening it, until it had given up.

'Enough!' Sam shouted at himself inwardly. 'It

isn't as bad as that. Don't let them get to you. It's just a stupid, childish game.'

'Penny for them.'

Sam spun round and nearly fell off the gate. 'Dad, what are you doing here?'

'Finished early. You must have been miles away not to hear me coming. Isn't it a bit cold to be sitting out here?'

'I was just thinking about the war,' said Sam quickly, glad to be able to change the subject. 'I mean, nothing's happening is it, nothing we need to worry about anyway.'

'We're not off the hook yet, son, even if people are beginning to call it the Bore War.'

'Snore war more like,' sniggered Sam. 'Can't do much else in a blackout.'

'Hitler and his bullies won't stop until we've all surrendered, except that we're not going to,' continued his father, ignoring the joke. 'Now, do you want to hop on the back or are you going to walk the rest of the way?'

Sam jumped up behind his father and held on tight.

As soon as they were home, Arthur disappeared down the garden to feed his pigeons while it was still daylight. Sam thought about offering to help, to make an effort, but his mother sent him off to tidy his room which she said looked as though a bomb had hit it.

When he came downstairs again, his parents were talking in lowered tones and stopped when he entered the room. Sam waited for an explanation. It didn't come. His father went upstairs to change, then put on his coat and went out, just as Clare was delivered back from a friend's.

'Daddy!' she cried. 'Where are you going?'

'To see a man about a dog,' he smiled, ruffling her hair. 'Be a good girl for Mummy.'

'What dog?' she cried, but the spluttering of the motorcycle drowned out her question.

'Why has Daddy gone to see a man about a dog?' she asked as she came into the kitchen. 'Are we getting one?'

'Nitwit, nitwit,' chanted Sam.

'It's just an expression, love,' said Hetty. 'It means he doesn't want to tell you where he's going.'

'Is the dog supposed to be a surprise then?'

Sam hooted with laughter. 'Dimbo, dumbo, dimmy, dummy, dumbo,' he sang. Clare began to whimper.

'Stop it, Sam,' rebuked his mother. 'Don't be so unkind.'

But Sam couldn't stop. He was gripped by a kind of hysteria, by a need to take out his anguish on someone else. By a need to hurt. 'Dimbo, dumbo, dimbo, dumbo,' he sang over and over.

'Go to your room, Sam,' Hetty ordered, 'and don't come down until you are ready to apologise.'

Sam tore upstairs and slammed his bedroom door behind him. For a while, he lay on the bed in the darkness hating everything: his mother, his sister, his father, the blackout, the pigeons, his tormentors. He felt suffocated by them all. He wanted to run away and hide where no one could find him, nothing could touch him. 'Leave me alone,' he whispered through the dark. 'Leave me alone.'

Eventually, he calmed himself down and switched on the light. He wasn't ready to go downstairs yet, to apologise. He wasn't in the mood for Clare's childish prattle. He would stay in his room and do some drawing until supper time.

He reached into his satchel for his pencil-case. Something sharp pricked the palm of his hand. Puzzled, he reached in further and felt something soft and tickly. He closed his hand round it and pulled it out. It was a feather. A grey pigeon's feather. Sam's heart somersaulted. How? How had a pigeon's feather got into his satchel? Could Clare have put it there? Sam knew that she hadn't. They had put it there. When he wasn't looking. They had put it there. Peck, peck, peck.

Sam grabbed his scissors from his pencil-case and frantically cut the feather into tiny pieces, tiny, tiny pieces, each cut an attempt to erase it from his mind and deny its existence. He was so intent on what he was doing that he didn't notice his mother come into the room. He flinched when she spoke.

'Do you want to talk, Sam?'

'Nothing to talk about.'

'I think there is. You were very unkind again to Clare. That's not like you. Is something bothering you?'

'She's annoying.'

'This isn't about Clare though, is it?' said his mother.

'Where's Dad gone?' said Sam, refusing to be drawn.

'Your father's joining the National Pigeon Service. That means that our pigeons will be used in the war effort.'

'Hitler *will* be scared,' said Sam with all the sarcasm he could muster.

Hetty ignored him and continued, 'They'll be used to carry messages back from the front line.'

'What's wrong with the wireless?' sniggered Sam.

'Dad could use some help with the pigeons, what with Matt being away, and I shall be working longer hours at the hospital.'

'No way,' yelled Sam. 'I hate them.'

'We're all doing our bit, Sam.'

'I'd rather grow potatoes,' snarled Sam.

'Perhaps we can talk about this again when you're in a better mood,' said his mother quietly, and she left the room.

Her voice went round and round in Sam's head,

the disappointment in it, the puzzlement. 'We're all doing our bit, Sam.'

Yeah, they were all doing their bit all right. They were all doing their bit to finish him off.

# CHAPTER SIX

On St Valentine's Day, it started with a vengeance.
Nothing had happened since the feather-in-the-
satchel episode and Sam, exhausted from being con-
stantly on his guard, relaxed enough to join in with
the classroom banter about who had sent what and
to whom. Two envelopes lay in his desk tempting
him to explore their secret contents, but he wasn't
going to open them in front of prying eyes. Sam
blushed with delight at the fact that two girls in his
class found him attractive enough to want to send
him a card. He wondered who they were. He scruti-
nised his classmates in the hope of spotting a clue,
but it was a time of bravado and deceit, bluff and
double-bluff, with some of them pretending they had
sent and received half a dozen cards each. At least he

hadn't been left out on what could be an isolating day for those who had.

It was lunchtime before he managed to sneak the envelopes into his pocket and disappear across the schoolyard into the boys' toilets.

'What a place to read love letters,' he grinned to himself wryly as he locked himself in a cubicle and sat down on the seat. He looked at his name – MASTER SAMUEL LONSDALE – on the first envelope, the thick, square, capital letters giving nothing away of the writer's identity. He tore open the envelope and pulled out a handmade card, beautifully illustrated on the front with painted flowers, and on the inside a single decorated line of text saying, 'SMILE AND BE MY VALENTINE'. Sam smiled instantly, he couldn't help himself, a great big beam of a smile. Who could it be? Who wanted to be his Valentine?

He picked up the other envelope from his lap. TO SAM LONSDALE it read, in capital letters again, but spidery and sloping slightly. He tore it open and pulled out the card. A cut-out black-and-white photograph of a pigeon was stuck on the front. Inside, was a drawing of a pigeon with a drawn arrow piercing its heart and the letters A.L. at both ends of the arrow.

Sam broke out in a cold sweat and shook uncontrollably. The moment of sheer joy he had felt only two minutes ago was replaced by sheer agony. He ripped the card in two and threw it on the ground, then he picked the pieces up again and screwed them up into tiny balls. He hurled them into the toilet and pulled the chain, but they bobbed back to the surface when the water had finished running.

He waited in desperation for the cistern to refill, then he pulled the chain again as hard as he could. As he did so, a voice from the next cubicle called, 'Cooooeee, having trouble in there?'

'Go away!' screamed Sam. 'Leave me alone!'

'He wants to be left alone. How tweet!' came a voice from the other side.

'Why are you doing this?' shrieked Sam. 'It's not my fault if my dad—' He stopped, but too late. The Judas-kiss had escaped from his lips.

'If your dad fancies pigeons, is that it? And him a married man, too.'

'You're sick,' cried Sam.

'Not half as sick as your dad. He'll be building a love nest next.'

'How tweet, tweet, tweet!'

Howls of laughter assaulted Sam from both sides. He had to get away. He slid back the lock, flung open the door and hurtled across the schoolyard. A voice called after him, 'Oh, Romeo, you left your love letters behind.'

Sam ran to his empty classroom and sat down at his desk, head in hands. How could he have done that? How could he have betrayed his father so easily? It was all so stupid, stupid, stupid. They were twisting words to fit their own malicious games, but there wasn't a shred of truth behind their accusations. If he knew that, why couldn't he treat it all with the contempt that it deserved? Why hadn't he supported his father instead of betraying him?

'You shouldn't be in here, Lonsdale. Is something wrong?'

Sam's form teacher stood at the doorway of the classroom.

'No, sir. I've got a bit of a headache, that's all, sir.'

The teacher came and stood by the desk and

looked at Sam carefully.

'Are you sure there's nothing worrying you, nothing you want to talk about? Your work's been going downhill recently, and you don't appear to be paying much attention in class.'

'How long do you think the war's going to go on, sir?' asked Sam.

'Difficult to say. It could be a few months, it could be less, it could be more. Depends who gives up first and when. It would be nice to get back to normal though, wouldn't it?'

Sam couldn't remember what normal was any more.

'Leave the worrying to the grown-ups, Lonsdale. It's their mess, not yours. You just make the most of your time here. You won't get a second chance.'

The school bell rang and Sam was spared any further awkward questions. His classmates barged their way back into the classroom, loud and boisterous, and Sam was suddenly aware of the gulf that was developing between himself and even his closest friends. He wasn't like them now. He no longer shared their natural exuberance, which remained undimmed even by the fear of war, and he was cut off from them by secret torments which were his and his alone to bear. It wouldn't be long before his friends recognised the gulf as well and drifted away from him. Sam wondered how long it would be before he became a total outcast.

# CHAPTER SEVEN

Sam tried to keep out of their way as much as possible over the next few weeks, setting his sights on the Easter holidays, when Matt was due back and he wouldn't have to worry about them for a while. He took longer and longer walking to school in the mornings, to put off the moment when he would have to pass through the gates and possibly see them leering at him across the playground. He was late several times and began to get into trouble with his teacher, but at least when he was late he knew he wouldn't bump into them.

In the afternoons, if he could he would dash out of the classroom ahead of anyone else, then hare out of school and along the road out of the village. Or he would take a circuitous route, heading out of school in the opposite direction and following the back lanes round until they met up with his own road beyond the church.

That didn't stop them from putting eggs in his satchel which broke when Sam unwittingly threw his books in on top. It didn't stop them from leaving crude notes in his desk. It didn't stop them from shouting out behind him, 'Get that dirty vermin off the pitch!' when a wood pigeon flew down in the middle of a football match near where Sam was playing in goal. And as if that wasn't enough, they then sat down on the grass just behind the net and cooed and burbled right the way through the second half of the match, not loudly enough for anyone else to hear, but sufficient to make Sam muck up two easy saves and earn the wrath of his team-mates.

At last the Easter holidays arrived, and with them a change in the weather. The freezing cold winter days were replaced almost overnight by a heatwave. The depressing news about the war in Europe gave way to stories of crowded beaches and people determined to go out and enjoy themselves come what may. Sam relaxed into the general mood of optimism that took hold. Mr Humphreys asked if he would like to help with lambing, and he set off every day to the neighbouring farm, where his greatest thrill was being allowed to bottle-feed a new-born lamb that had been rejected by its mother. He lay down in the straw, with the lamb tucked under one arm, and watched with triumph as it sucked and pulled at the teat until the milk had all gone. It became known as Sam's Lamb and followed him around as soon as he arrived at the farm each day.

At home, his father was engrossed in matching up his pigeons. He had agreed to set up a breeding programme to help ensure a continuous supply of young, trainable birds to the armed forces. One of the things he prided himself on in peace time was matching the right males with the right females to produce top-class racing youngsters.

'That's half the fun of it,' he said, 'to create a winning mix.'

'What does it matter, if you're not going to race them?' asked Sam.

'It matters a lot,' Arthur laughed. 'I don't want to be responsible for sending the forces a whole lot of birds that can't make the distance. A right fool I'd look if they all flopped down into the Channel before they'd even reached England!'

Over the next few days, Sam watched his father take down the pigeons' box-perches and replace them with nest-boxes lined with sand. Into each nest-box, Arthur placed a cock bird and, as soon as the cocks were all settled, he gave each one a hen.

'What if they don't like each other?' sniggered Sam, as he watched one pair of birds eyeing each other beadily. 'Was that what happened to the pigeon that died?'

'Sometimes a weaker bird, male or female, is picked on by a dominant male. You have to keep an eye on them and nip any bullying in the bud. It's my fault if I don't see what's going on. It's only ever happened once, and it won't happen again.'

The first ten days of the holidays passed and Matt didn't come home. There was still no word from him, either. Sam grew anxious about the prospect of going back to school without talking to his brother. Easter itself became a muted affair. It had been the custom for Matt to blow a dozen eggs and paint them with elaborate patterns, helped by Sam and Clare. It was Matt, too, who bought and hid chocolate eggs all round the garden for everyone else to find, not that there were many to be bought this year, except at exorbitant prices. Hetty had planned a special meal for when they returned from church on Sunday, but no one felt like celebrating.

It wasn't until the last day of the holidays that a letter arrived from Matt. Arthur read it out after Clare had gone to bed.

*Dear Everyone Back Home,*

*I'm afraid I'm not going to make it back for Easter after all. And I was so looking forward to Mum's cooking. I'm tramping around somewhere between Abbeville and Arras. Rumour has it that the Germans aren't that far away, but we haven't seen one yet. They're not dishing out leave at the moment. They're not dishing out anything much, actually. Our supplies seem to have got held up somewhere. We've been living off stewed dandelions and nettles for the past two days, and the lice have been living off us for the past few weeks! Oh, for a soak in a tub of hot water! If I look anything like my fellow soldiers, I am a fright for sore eyes. You'd have a fit, Mum.*

*I'm with a great crowd of lads, though our sergeant's a bit of a sourpuss – aren't they all?*

*I hope everything's all right at home and that you're not worrying too much. I can't say when they'll allow us some leave. Seems we might be needed to fight a rear-guard action if the Germans keep pushing forward, though they must surely run out of steam soon.*

*Lots of love, and take care, Matt*

'Thank goodness he's safe,' said Hetty. 'I can cope with not seeing him as long as I know he's all right.'

Sam was delighted to know that Matt was safe, but he felt as though he was alone in a yacht lost in treacherous seas, with no prospect of rescue because the search for him had been called off. The holidays were at an end, he was going back to school, things were bound to get worse, and there was no one to help.

# CHAPTER EIGHT

Hetty was beginning to work longer hours at the hospital. The remorseless advance of the German army across Europe brought the threat of war closer and closer to home. Every hospital in the country was taking in more beds, stocking up with emergency supplies, and dealing with fewer non-urgent cases.

'I'm going to have to work late today,' she announced over breakfast, soon after the new term had begun, 'so can you go in by bicycle please, Sam? I've arranged for Clare to stay on at school, and they'll pop her over the road so that she can cycle back with you.'

'No!' Sam protested loudly. 'I don't want to. I can't. I've got cricket practice.'

'Then Clare can watch you until you've finished,' said Hetty.

'I don't want to watch him.'

'And I don't want her watching me.'

'That's enough, the pair of you,' Arthur intervened. 'Your mother's asked you to do something, and you'll do it. End of discussion.'

Sam glared at his father, got up from the table and stormed out of the room. *Great. Just great.* They would have a field day with him now. Something else for them to get their teeth into. He pulled open the front door, slammed it behind him, and realised only then that it was pouring with rain. Tough. He jumped on to his bike and cycled furiously away, deliberately riding through every puddle he came to. Half a mile down the road, he remembered that he had forgotten his school bag with his homework, and that meant more trouble with his teachers. Well, he wasn't going back. He cycled on, taking the long route round the outer edge of the village to make sure that he wasn't early.

By the time Sam reached school, he was soaked through and the last of the stragglers were already disappearing through the door. He took his bicycle to the shed and, as he turned round towards the school building, he saw one of them staring at him from an upstairs window; staring at him, then waving at him. Sam looked away and strode quickly across the playground. Don't let him see you run.

'Making a bit of a habit of this, aren't you, Lonsdale? And wouldn't it be sensible to wear appropriate clothing in this sort of weather?'

The Head, just inside the door, waiting to pounce.

'Yes, Sir, sorry, Sir.'

'Too many late nights is it, Lonsdale? Can't get up in the morning?'

'No, Sir.'

'What, then? Your work's been slipping too, I hear.'

'Sorry, Sir.'

'Pull yourself together then, lad. Can't have you letting the side down, can we?'

'Yes, Sir, no, Sir.'

Sam escaped gratefully to his classroom, only to find himself in more trouble for missing the first ten minutes of a geography test. He sat uncomfortably at his desk, trousers and shirt clinging wet and cold, and tried to focus on cloud types and formations. Which were the ones like cotton wool? Which ones carried rain? Words like nimbus and cumulus floated around, but he hadn't a clue what they meant. Moreover, he didn't care, except that one of them had contributed towards his current soggy state. He gazed round the room at his classmates scribbling away, and earned himself another rebuke from the teacher, who thought he might be trying to cheat. I don't care enough to cheat, Sir.

Lessons in science, mathematics and English followed. Sam was reprimanded for failing to pay attention in science, and for failing to bring in his homework in mathematics.

'Perhaps we should send you home to fetch it, Lonsdale,' said his teacher, 'then we'd find out if you've actually done it.'

In English, he was mortified when, as a punishment for being unable to produce his own poem about the spring, he was made to recite 'April Days', by Robert Loveman.

The poet's name was enough to set off a wave of

titters round the classroom, but when he began: 'It isn't raining rain to me, It's raining daffodils', several of the evacuees sniggered out loud. By the time he'd reached the closing lines of: 'A health unto the happy, A fig for him who frets – It isn't raining rain to me, It's raining violets', the whole class was falling about with laughter, despite the teacher's efforts to re-establish order.

'Smashin'!' one of the evacuees shouted. 'Spoke with real feelin'.'

'So it was daffodils what made you wet this morning, or was it violets?'

'A fig for you, mate.'

'Funny fings 'appen in the countryside, don't they, Sir?'

'SILENCE! This isn't a cattle market.'

'There's a few beefbrains in 'ere though, ain't there, Sir?'

This final remark brought more sniggers from the evacuees but, as the rest of the class digested what had been said, their teacher regained control. Sam was at last able to sit down and watch the spotlight fall on someone else.

When the bell rang for lunch, Sam pushed his way out of the room before anyone could poke more fun at him. To his amazement though, as he queued to get his food, he found himself surrounded by friends and a number of other children from his class, all of whom were sympathising with him over his mauling at the hands of 'those pig-ignorant vacks'. Mostly, Sam knew, they were enraged at being called beef-brains, but suddenly he was at the centre of an 'anti-vack' movement, with two of his friends whipping up hostility, using the evacuees' mockery of him as justification for a fight.

Sam was appalled. He didn't want this. He hadn't enjoyed being laughed at, however there had been nothing vicious about it, and he knew very well that his friends had been laughing at him too. 'Leave me out of it,' he wanted to yell, but to do that would have been to isolate himself still further. The mood of the class had swung too far: they wanted this fight. They expected the natives to show solidarity against the intruders, and they expected Sam to be their figurehead as they prepared to do battle on his behalf. Moreover, they were encouraging support from other classes.

By the time Sam and his friends spilled out of the dining room into the playground, a crowd had gathered, whose minor grievances against the evacuees were shared and embellished, added to the beefbrain episode and the outrageous treatment of Sam, until nothing could prevent outright war. The evacuees, meanwhile, sensing from the whispered comments and dagger looks a drastic worsening in attitude towards them, began to group themselves defensively on the other side of the playground.

When the on-duty teacher disappeared round the back of the school building to check the bicycle-sheds and lavatories, the first salvoes were launched.

'Why don't you go back to where you belong, you ignorant, flea-ridden vermin?'

'Yeh, we don't want you here. You're just a bunch of snotty-nosed troublemakers.'

There was a moment of quiet amongst the evacuees as they shuffled uncomfortably and wondered who would dare to be their spokesman. Then a voice shouted back, 'We didn't ask to come to this dump. Do you think we enjoy living with a herd of boneheads and waking to the smell of dung every morning?'

All around him, Sam felt the raw fury of his class-mates, and suddenly it excited him, thrilled him. He wasn't on his own any more. He had been wronged, his friends had been wronged, they were supporting him, he was one of them. Down with the vacks. Send them all home. He began to push forward and the crowd pushed forward with him. He wasn't a victim. He was in control.

'You've asked for it now, scum,' someone yelled.

'Get them,' someone else cried.

Get them, get them.

'If you wanna fight, we're ready, numbskulls.'

'Yeh, what yer waitin' for?'

Get them, get them.

Some instinct for survival made Sam hang back, as the more fist-happy members of the two mobs launched themselves at each other with a hail of punches. Their supporters cheered and urged them on, finding a welcome release for months of pent-up fears and anxieties. And then, as the punches drew blood and one of the girls began to scream, Sam didn't want to be there. He was catapulted back to the stark reality of what they were doing, and a shiver of revulsion ran down his spine. He turned to move away, just as the on-duty teacher reappeared. He registered the look of horror on her face, and felt thoroughly ashamed of himself and his cohorts.

'Stop it, this minute,' she shouted, but no one could hear her above the clamour of the crowd.

Sam nudged those closest to him, as the teacher tried again to make herself heard. Very slowly, through a network of prods and hisses, the message went round that the ceasefire had sounded. Bodies swivelled to check out the unwelcome figure of authority, then stood awkwardly to attention. A few frontline fighters were reluctant to lower their fists, but even they were powerless to resist the all-enveloping silence that spread across the playground.

The teacher left them to suffer their awkwardness for a few moments, gazing at them eagle-eyed, memorising names and bloody faces.

'What do you think you were doing?' she said at last. 'This is a school playground, not a war zone.'

Most of those involved kept their eyes fixed to the ground, but one of the evacuees from Sam's class stepped forward, and for a moment Sam thought he was going to point the finger of blame at him for sparking the trouble.

'We was just 'avin' a bit of a lark, Miss. No 'arm done.'

The teacher stared at the evacuee's swollen lip and bloody nose.

'No harm done? If your mother were here, what do you think she would say if I sent you home looking like that?'

'Don't know, Miss. She'd probably say it served me right.'

Sam was amazed at the boy's willingness to shoulder responsibility for what had happened, but it wasn't right. Nothing the evacuees had done warranted such an attack. There had been name-calling ever since they had arrived, but it was just banter and both sides gave as good as they got. No one had ever felt threatened by it.

'Fighting, in any shape or form, will not be tolerated in school,' the teacher continued. 'At a time like this, we should be pulling together. It is a difficult time for all of us, and especially those of you who are a long way from home. But that doesn't excuse the sort of behaviour I have just witnessed. I shall expect all of you who were involved, whether in fighting or cheering, to stay behind for detention tomorrow evening.'

She finished speaking, and Sam looked up, ready to move away. Just as he did so, he saw them, hovering at the back of the group of evacuees. They stared straight at him and grinned, then swaggered off across the playground. How long had they been there? Long enough to see him cheering, shoving, chanting? Clever enough not to get themselves involved in anything so public. But they were up to something. Sam was desperate for the misery of this school day to be over, yet he dreaded what he was going to find once the bell had sounded and he was on his way home.

The afternoon continued with further reprimands for inattention, but Sam scarcely noticed as he watched the minutes ticking by. The final lesson came to an end with a loud clattering of desk lids and scraping of chairs, and as everyone pushed noisily towards the door, the school secretary came in with

Clare by her side, sucking her thumb. Oh joy.

'There you are, dear. Your brother will look after you now.'

The minute she saw Sam, Clare bustled over to him and grabbed his hand. Thank you, God. Thank you. Sam yanked her quickly out of the classroom before she could say anything to embarrass him, then pulled his hand out of hers and walked quickly along the corridor and down the stairs.

'Wait for me, wait, Sammy,' she cried. 'Don't go so fast.'

He carried on, out through the front doors and across the playground towards the bike-sheds. It wasn't until he was right up close that he saw what they had done, and at that moment Clare, running to catch up with him, tripped over and began to scream. Sam turned to look at her shaking body on the ground and then back to his flat-tyred, feather-enhanced bicycle. He stood there helplessly, and felt nothing but a sickening emptiness inside. He heard his name being called and ignored it. The second time was more commanding, but still Sam ignored it. Then he found himself being forced round by the shoulder to face his biology teacher.

'What is it with you, Lonsdale? You pay no attention in class, and now you refuse to answer when you're called.'

'Sorry, Sir.'

'Your sister's cut her knee and I've sent her to have it bandaged. You'd better go and fetch her from the office.'

'Yes, Sir.'

As Sam started to walk away, the teacher caught him by the arm.

'Is that your bicycle, Lonsdale?'

'Yes, Sir.'

'And do you know who's responsible for the state it's in?'

'No, Sir.'

The teacher peered at him closely, but Sam kept his eyes fixed to the ground.

'Would you like me to do a bit of enquiring?'

'No, Sir, thank you, Sir. I expect someone's just having a bit of fun.'

'I don't call that funny, more like vandalism, and if I find out who was responsible, they'll have feathers coming out of their backside.'

'Yes, Sir.'

Sam couldn't resist a smirk as the teacher marched off across the playground. He quickly plucked the feathers from the chain and unstuck them from the seat and handlebars, then wheeled the bicycle over to the school building. Clare was just being shown out.

'You were going too fast, Sammy,' she said accusingly. 'I said to you not to but you didn't listen. I felled over and cut my knee.'

'Well I didn't ask to take you home, did I? Stop whingeing and go and get your bike.'

'I don't like you, Samuel Lonsdale. I'm going to tell Mummy of you.'

Sam's only concern was to get home without being caught. Would they have given up waiting for him by now? That was the only hope he had. He set off at a brisk pace, pushing his bicycle, with Clare pedalling away just behind him. As her legs began to tire, he had to stop every so often to give her a rest. He tutted irritably, watching all the time for them to appear. And then, as they reached the War Memorial by the village pond, he heard the first 'Coooeeee!'

Clare stopped pedalling and looked round.

'What was that, Sammy?' she asked.

'Never mind,' snapped Sam. 'Keep cycling.'

Three heads suddenly poked out from behind the War Memorial.

'Coooooeeee! Sammy!' all three of them called together.

Clare began to giggle. 'Your friends are being silly,' she said. 'They sound just like our pigeons.'

They came round the front of the Memorial, whooping and cooing, and began to wave feathers in the air while they performed some sort of tribal dance.

'Where are your feathers, Sam? We left you lots.'

Sam wheeled his bike past them and shouted angrily to Clare, who had stopped to watch, 'Keep cycling, I said. Just ignore them.'

'I want to go and play with them,' Clare said stubbornly.

'Well you can't,' yelled Sam. 'We're going home.'

'You're such a spoilsport, Samuel Lonsdale. I hate you, I hate you.'

'I hate you, I hate you,' they mimicked, and they

danced off down the road, waving their feathers and cooing over and over again.

That was enough for Sam. He made up his mind there and then that he wasn't going back to school. He waited for Clare to catch up with him, and they made their way home in silence.

# CHAPTER NINE

Sam woke and stared into the blackness of his room. He could hear his mother clattering plates and cutlery in the kitchen, while Clare chattered to her nonstop. From the garden he could hear his father whistling and the rumble of the wheelbarrow on the path. The sounds of an ordinary morning, but this was no ordinary morning.

Sam had already planned what he was going to do. Arthur had repaired the tyres on his bicycle, but he had to make sure that Hetty wouldn't ask him to take Clare with him. He also had to make sure that no one saw him go off in the wrong direction. That meant that he needed to leave the house earlier than usual, and too early to take Clare. Instead of waiting to be turfed out of bed, Sam leapt to his feet and quickly pulled on his school clothes, then bolted downstairs and into the kitchen.

'Goodness gracious me!' Hetty exclaimed. 'I must be seeing things.' She wiped her hand across her brow as though she were going to faint.

'Is breakfast ready, Mum? I'm in a hurry.'

'What are you doing up, Samuel Lonsdale?' demanded Clare. 'You never get up till you're told to, does he, Mummy?'

'Mind your own business, snotty nose,' snapped Sam, and was delighted to see his sister wipe her nose on her sleeve in response.

'That's enough of that sort of language, young man. Anyway, why are you in such a rush to get to school?'

'They're choosing the cricket team soon, so me and some of my friends want to get some extra practice in.'

Liar, liar, liar. Sam felt his cheeks going red. He picked up a loaf of bread and started to cut himself a piece so that his mother couldn't see his face.

'I didn't know you were so keen,' said Hetty. 'Football, cricket, goodness me.'

Sam's father came in then, and Sam felt himself blushing all over again as his mother repeated the reasons he had given for his early appearance.

'Better tuck into a big breakfast then, Sam,' said Arthur. 'You need to stoke up those energy levels or you'll never make it through such a long day.'

'Ha, ha, very funny, Dad.'

I wish it was funny, Dad, but it's not, because I've just told an absolute whopper of a lie, and I'm going to have to tell more lies because I'm not even going to school, let alone going to play cricket. Sam felt so guilty that it was a struggle to eat at all, but at last he finished everything that was put in front of him, threw his school bag over his shoulders, said goodbye, and went out through the front door. He set off on his bike in the direction of the school, but quickly did a U-turn along a narrow bridle-path, rejoining the road several hundred yards beyond his own house and the cluster of neighbouring houses and farm buildings; far enough away not to be recognised.

At first the chill morning air whipped through his thin school blazer as he cycled along, but Sam soon warmed up and the unwavering whirr of the wheels on the tarmac was curiously calming. His fears at the enormity of what he was doing gradually gave way to a tremendous feeling of freedom. He slowed down and, as the pale spring sun broke through the mist, he began to enjoy watching lambs gambolling across the fields and foals tottering around on their stick-thin legs. The hedgerows rustled with activity, and rabbits hopped out on to the road in front of him before bolting away as soon as he drew too close.

After about ten miles, Sam decided to stop and walk the rest of the way. He hid his cycle behind a hedge, and began the long trek down towards the beach.

He had gone only a short distance when, suddenly, he heard 'Cooee!' and froze in his steps. He looked round but there was no one there. Had he imagined it? It wouldn't be the first time. He was just about to run when he realised that it was a girl's voice he had heard. Did that mean a girl had joined them? Did that mean there was someone else to make his life a misery? Did it mean that they were now following him wherever he went?

'Hey, you, down there,' the voice called again. A strange accent.

Sam looked up into a shock of ginger curls. A girl, slightly older than himself, was sitting astride a large branch.

'You skiving off too?' she asked.

Sam didn't answer. He was too rattled. Anyway, it was none of her business.

'First tree I've ever climbed,' she said. 'Not sure I can get down again.'

Sam wanted to keep walking, but at the same time he was curious to know who the girl was and why, like him, she wasn't at school.

'You coming up?' she asked. 'You can see the sea from here, and no one can see us.'

Sam hesitated. This wasn't what he had planned. He wanted to be on his own, didn't he? Or did he? He glanced up and down the road, then grabbed hold of the lowest branch and began to climb. He sat himself on a branch that spread out at right angles to the one the girl was on.

'You looked dead scared when I called out to you,' she said. 'Like you'd been caught in a trap.'

'I wasn't expecting to be spoken to by a tree,' said Sam, half wondering if this might just be a trap.

The girl laughed out loud, making Sam peer anxiously down through the branches.

'This your first time?' she asked.

'Up a tree?'

'No, you nincompoop,' she laughed again. 'Skiving off, I meant.'

Sam shrugged his shoulders. 'What makes you think I'm skiving? Maybe everyone just got the day off.'

'We didn't though, did we? I go to the same school as you so I know we didn't. I've seen you there. Year below me.'

Sam stared at her, but couldn't remember having seen her before. She opened her jacket and, sure enough, she was wearing the same uniform.

'I'm one of those ignorant vacks who're cluttering up the classrooms spreading their nits,' she said without any hint of acrimony.

Sam involuntarily scratched his head. 'Who are you staying with?' he asked, for want of something better to say.

'Her name's Miss Dumpton. She's about ninety-two and four feet six inches, she's got a giant wart on the end of her nose and her house smells of Brussels sprouts.'

'Seriously?'

'The sprouts bit is very serious. The pong goes everywhere with me. I'm surprised you haven't fallen out of the tree because of it. She's all right, though. Bit eccentric. She keeps doves and talks to them as though they are her children.'

Sam felt the hairs prickle round the back of his neck.

'Don't you miss your family?' he asked, trying to keep the conversation away from himself.

'My dad's dead, long time ago. I miss my mum but I hate her new boyfriend, and my brother's in the army. I miss my friends. It's hard to make new friends, especially in a strange place where everyone takes the mickey 'cos you don't speak the same and don't know about the same things. Anyway, what's the point when you know you're not going to be around for very long?'

'Does it bother you, people taking the mickey?' asked Sam.

'It's their problem, not mine. It's not my fault if I haven't ever seen a tractor. They don't have them in cities. Doesn't make me any less of a person.'

'Well, you'll be able to go back and boast to your friends,' grinned Sam, 'because there's one in that field over there.'

The girl looked to where Sam was pointing. 'What are all those birds doing, flying along behind it?'

'They're seagulls. They're looking for worms and other titbits in the soil that's been dug up.'

'I thought seagulls only ate fish.'

'They'll eat anything. They're right scavengers.'

They sat watching for a while. Once again, Sam took in the enormity of what he was doing and his stomach turned to jelly.

'It's your turn to answer the questions now,' the girl broke into his thoughts. 'Are you bored, or are you being bullied?'

That was certainly direct. Sam felt himself blushing, but pretended not to understand.

'The two main reasons for skiving off school,' the girl explained.

Sam turned away and didn't answer.

81

'Bullied then,' said the girl. 'If you were bored, you'd say so.'

'Maybe I just wanted a day off,' retorted Sam fiercely. 'And I'm not going to spend it sitting up here.' He clambered down from the tree as quickly as he could, scraping his shin on the way, and marched off down the road.

'My name's Polly,' the girl called after him. 'Maybe see you tomorrow?'

'Maybe,' said Sam. 'Maybe not,' he muttered to himself.

Soon the road petered away into a steep, gravelly path. The sun vanished behind ominous grey clouds and the wind buffeted Sam as he trudged along. He leaned into it, pulling his blazer tightly round him and turning the collar up over his ears. He followed the path all the way down to the sea front, and then stood up straight to look around. He was startled to discover that a barrier of rolled barbed wire corkscrewed along the beach for as far as he could see. It was such a stark representation of the way in which the life of his country was being choked by the threat of invasion, that Sam could only stand and stare.

The sea was closed to him. Unreachable. Untouchable. No more leaping waves and skimming stones. No more gazing out at the sheer vastness of it and feeling the delicious sense of freedom that it aroused. Sam wanted to rip the wire away with his bare hands, march to the edge of the sea and dare the Germans to come and get it over with. Anything would be better than the waiting and not knowing. Anything would be better than being trapped behind this obscene barrier.

He walked down to the wire and touched one of the sharp points.

'Nasty stuff, eh?'

Sam spun round to see an Air Raid Precautions warden standing at the end of the path. He walked over to Sam. 'Got to keep Jerry out. Take him a while to snip his way through this lot.'

'Was it deliberately designed to tear through a person's skin?' asked Sam.

'I think it was used originally to separate cattle from sheep on the American prairies,' said the Air Raid Precautions warden. He peered closely at Sam. 'Aren't you Arthur Lonsdale's son?'

Sam quickly turned away. Couldn't he go anywhere without being recognised? He nodded reluctantly.

'I thought so. You were with him a little while ago, on your way to the market. No school today?'

Sam shook his head, aware that the man would have noticed his uniform, but offered no explanation. The man waited a few seconds, before continuing, 'He's a good man, your father. Won a medal for bravery in the First World War, didn't he? It's hard to be told you're too old to fight this time round. Even harder too to see your own kids going off in your place.'

Sam nodded. Medal for bravery? He didn't know that. He couldn't even imagine his father fighting. He wondered why he had never said anything about it.

'Just let them try coming over here, that's all I can say. Us oldies'll soon show 'em what's what.'

Sam smiled at the man's simple belief in his countrymen's superiority. 'I'd better go,' he said.

'Back to school tomorrow, then.' It wasn't a question, more an order. 'Got to keep things going, haven't we?'

Just for a brief moment, Sam thought about telling this man what was happening to him. But then, just as quickly, he dismissed the idea. There was a war on. His father was a war hero. Wouldn't this man tell him it was all a lot of nonsense and to grow up? Wouldn't he tell him that he was letting his father down? He said goodbye and began the walk back up the path.

'Find someone to talk to,' the man called after him. 'Talk to your father.'

No way, no bloomin' way, thought Sam as he walked back up the path and began the long climb up towards the road. To his relief, the girl had gone from the tree. He had had enough of being interrogated, and in any case he wanted to think about what the Air Raid Precautions warden had told him about his father.

# CHAPTER TEN

That night Sam dreamt that he was caught up in the middle of the roll of barbed wire. Pigeons were trying to get at him from one side and the Germans from the other. As long as he stayed in the middle he was safe. He walked along for mile after mile after mile, praying that he would reach a place where there would be no pigeons and no Germans, but they followed him all the way, thousands of them, swooping at him, wings and greatcoats spread like a blackout to block the light. He could bear it no longer. He would have to cut his way out and give himself up. But which side should he choose? He was just about to make a first cut when his father charged on to the beach. The moment the Germans saw his father they disappeared all in one go, and the pigeons, hearing his voice, flew up to the cliffs and perched there waiting for him to tell them what to do. Sam cut and tugged his way out of the barbed wire and hurtled up the beach into his father's arms. Safe at last.

'Are you going to school today?' Arthur asked.

Sam rubbed his eyes. 'Eh? What?' School? No! Not safe. Am I going? Does he know?

'School, Sam. It's time you were getting up.'

Sam felt the heavy weight of his father's hand on his shoulder. He wanted to pull his arm all the way round him and keep it there. But he didn't. He turned over and sat up. 'Where's Mum?'

'Clare's come up in a rash. Mum's taken her to the doctor. If you like, I'll take you to school on the motorcycle. I'm meeting someone in the village.'

Think, quick. 'It's all right, Dad. You go ahead. I said I'd catch up with one of my friends on the way.'

How easily the lies suggested themselves, blotted out the truth and took over. Sam blushed with guilt, and regretted that yet again he was rejecting his father's hand of friendship. The blush conveyed an accidental deceit.

'Girl friend, is it?' his father grinned. 'Well, I wouldn't want to play gooseberry. Up you get then, or you'll be late.'

Arthur went downstairs and Sam scrambled into his school clothes. He didn't like this pretence. Why couldn't he just talk to his father like the Air Raid Precautions warden had said? There was nobody else in the house: it was the perfect moment. But breakfast came and went with chat about the change in the weather, and then his father seized the moment from him.

'Sam, I know you don't want anything to do with the pigeons, and why should you, it's my hobby after all. But I could do with some help.'

Sam grimaced but said nothing.

'It sounds ridiculous, I know, but the army, the air force, even the intelligence services are using pigeons to carry messages, and they need more and more of them. If Matt was here, I'd ask him, but he isn't and I could use an extra pair of hands.'

The perfect opportunity to step into Matt's shoes, the perfect opportunity to make amends to his father. Take it, take it! Sam remained silent.

'Perhaps one of your friends would like to help as well.' Friends? Sam wasn't sure he had any any more.

'They can save lives, these birds,' persuaded his father. 'That's why they're so important.'

They can ruin lives, too, thought Sam. 'Did you fight in the First World War, Dad?' he asked suddenly.

'Just for a short time. I was too young at the beginning.'

'Did you win a medal?'

Arthur Lonsdale looked questioningly at his son. 'Yes, but I didn't deserve it any more than anyone else. Everyone who fights for their country deserves a medal.'

It was so typical of his father to play down his role. Sam knew he ought to admire his humility, but right now he wanted him to blow a trumpet, bang on a big bass drum and shout from the rooftops about what he had done. 'What was the medal for?' he urged.

'I rescued three of our platoon from a burning building. Anyone else would have done the same.'

'What, you went back in three times?'

'Something like that. Anyway, it's time we were

off. Think about it, Sam. I won't force you, but I promise as soon as the war's over you won't have to go near those dratted birds again.'

Sam nodded and went to bring his cycle round to the front of the house. His father coaxed his motorcycle into life, waved to Sam and spluttered off down the road towards the village. Sam waited until he was out of sight, then set off in the opposite direction.

As he cycled along, Sam found himself hoping to bump into Polly again. He certainly wouldn't be going anywhere near the beach. The Air Raid Precautions warden would probably keep quiet about yesterday, but he would surely believe it was his duty to report a second encounter. It was a glorious spring morning and Sam felt his spirits lifting with every turn of the wheels. He would help his father. That was the least he could do. He would step into Matt's shoes. Keep things going until Matt came home. That's what Matt would have wanted, too.

Did Matt know their father was a hero? Sam tried to imagine what it would be like going into a burning building to save someone. The suffocating smoke. The searing heat. The terrifying flames. He didn't think he could do it. He realised with a pang that he didn't really know his father, had always thought of him as someone rather remote, too quiet, weak even. And yet he had saved the lives of three people. Sam's judgement of his father, he saw now, was based upon what Sam believed other people thought of him. No, not other people, what those boys thought of him. How could he have got to the point where his own feelings for his father were so terribly affected by what *they* said about him? Why was he allowing it to happen? If only he could be like Matt. 'Don't let the midges bite!' Well, he had let them bite, all over. He had let Matt down, and his father, and himself. But not any more. He would help his father, and Matt would be proud of him.

Sam freewheeled down a hill. As he reached the bottom, he heard a voice call, 'Hey, Mr Skiver, over here.'

He slowed down and saw Polly's face peering through a hedge.

'There's a gap just down there you can squeeze through. I promise not to ask any awkward questions. Cross my heart and hope to die, punch my nose if I tell a lie.'

Sam checked that no one was looking, then crawled through the gap and laid his bicycle on the ground. A rolling meadow, spattered with spring flowers, stretched out before him, bordered in a sweeping curve by dense woodland. Polly was sitting on a blanket, drinking from an enamel mug.

'Tea?' she asked.

'Is the kettle on?' smirked Sam.

'Ha, bloomin' ha,' she said, aiming a kick in his direction.

'How did you manage the blanket and tea?' asked Sam.

'Blind as a bat, old Miss Dumpton. I could walk out with all her silver and she wouldn't notice. The good news is there's a shortage of Brussels sprouts. The bad news is she's turned to cabbage instead, boiled until it's all mushy, see-through and very stinky.'

'Yeh, you do pong a bit,' snorted Sam.

Polly jumped to her feet and chased him across the meadow. 'I don't even know your name, you disgusting piece of mouldy cheese,' she yelled.

'Rumpelstiltskin,' he shouted, and she chased him harder still until, exhausted, she flopped back down on the blanket.

'Tea now, sir?' She held out a flask and the mug.

Sam took them and perched shyly on the edge of the blanket. 'My name's Sam, since you asked so nicely.'

'Delighted to meet you, young Sam,' said Polly pompously. 'And what brings you here on this extraordinarily beautiful spring day?'

'That's not an awkward question is it, because if it is I might have to punch you on the nose.' Sam held up a clenched fist and grinned. He found that he could relax and be himself with Polly. Not only that, but he felt the delicious sense of freedom that comes when you have made a decision about something that has been bothering you for months.

'I know the answer anyway,' Polly continued just as pompously. 'You couldn't resist another encounter with the fascinating and mesmerisingly beautiful Pollyanna. And who can blame you?'

'I couldn't resist another day off school, more like.'

'But you need to keep at it, my boy. You country bumpkins are a year behind us townies in most subjects, no offence of course.'

'You don't know much about what goes on outside your grimy old towns though, do you?' Sam countered good-humouredly.

'That's why I'm sitting up trees and in fields and not dying of boredom in a sweaty, nit-infested classroom.'

'Aren't you scared they'll find out?'

'Miss Dumpton wrote a letter to the school. "Dear Headmaster, I'm afraid poor Pollyanna has taken to her bed with the most frightful bout of influenza and won't be attending school for at least two weeks, quite possibly a month."'

Sam looked at Polly in astonishment. She grinned back at him.

'Do you want me to do one for you?'

Sam blushed and laughed, but suddenly fear spread through him like a poison. What had he got himself into? He had tried not to think about the consequences of missing school. His only thought had been that he could never go back again, beyond that nothing. But of course, sooner or later the school would question why he wasn't there and why they had received no explanation for his absence. Sooner or later they would contact his parents. His parents would be shocked to the core when they found out that he had been truanting; worse, that he had been lying to them. And then he would have to tell them why. What, then, was the alternative? At least if he accepted Polly's offer, it would give him some time before it all blew up in his face, even if in the end it just made things worse. And he knew that he could never write the letter himself.

'What's your dad like?' asked Polly. 'Will he go mad if he finds out you've been missing school?'

''Course he will.'

'What if you told him why? Would he understand?'

'I can't tell him,' snapped Sam. 'Shut up now, just shut up, will you?'

'I'm only trying to help,' said Polly quietly.

They sat in silence. A big black cloud spread heavy shadows across the meadow and a chill breeze served as a reminder that it was still only early spring.

'Someone's switched the sun off,' shivered Sam, trying to lighten the atmosphere.

Polly remained silent. Sam shifted awkwardly on the blanket, then suddenly he found himself blurting out, 'My dad won a medal in the last war.'

Polly turned to look at him. 'I bet you're proud of him.'

'Yeh,' said Sam. 'I suppose I am. He didn't tell me, you know. He doesn't even really want to talk about it.'

'Perhaps it makes him think about things he'd rather forget. It must be horrible seeing your friends being killed all around you.'

Sam hadn't thought about that. He had only imagined the glory of his father's act, a single triumphant moment divorced from any reality. Perhaps his father could only look back and see the horror of the reality.

'He keeps pigeons.'

There. It was out. No warning. No time to gulp it back. He stared across the meadow waiting for Polly's reaction.

'My uncle keeps chickens,' she said.

Sam collapsed with hysterical laughter. 'You can't race chickens,' he screeched. 'They can't fly!'

'They can run,' pouted Polly, and they both fell about laughing at the thought of a flock of chickens hurtling round a track.

'My dad's pigeons are going to spy for England,' boasted Sam.

'My uncle's chickens are going to die for England,' rejoined Polly. Then, 'What do you mean they're going to spy for England?'

'They're going to be used to carry messages to and from our troops overseas.'

'Can they fly that far?'

''Course they can. They can fly hundreds of miles and still find their way home.'

'That's amazing. Where does your dad keep them?'

'In a loft at the end of the garden.'

Sam paused and wondered again if he could trust Polly. She had responded so far without a hint of ridicule or condemnation, but she could be storing it all up to use against him later. But then why should she just because they did? Not everyone was like them.

'Some people think keeping pigeons is weird,' he tested the ground. 'They think pigeons are dirty and smelly and should be shot.'

'Some people are dirty and smelly and should be shot,' snorted Polly.

Sam was mildly shocked, but couldn't help muttering, 'I can think of three.'

'Same three as me, I expect,' said Polly.

Sam stared at her in utter bewilderment.

'Peter Simpkins, Arnold Tupper and Timothy Baldwin.'

Sam had always refused to say, even to think, their names. He felt he could maintain some vague sort of control over them if he refused to acknowledge their identities. If he didn't name them, he could at least try to pretend they were nobodies. Now their names hung in the air like a threatening storm waiting to engulf him.

'How did you know?' he murmured.

'I didn't,' said Polly, 'but I saw them following you once and you didn't look very happy. They're in my class. Creeps, all three of them.'

'They won't leave me alone. It's all stupid stuff,

about Dad's pigeons and how he fancies them, stupid stuff like that, but they just go on and on and on, and I don't know why I'm telling you because you'll probably think I'm pathetic, but I can't stand it because he's my dad and they make me feel ashamed of him.'

Sam scrambled to his feet and began to walk away across the meadow.

'Don't keep walking off,' Polly called after him.

Sam hesitated for a moment, then carried on.

'Do you love your dad?' Polly called again.

Sam spun round and glared at her. 'What's it to you?'

'Just that if you do, no one can touch that, and it doesn't matter how much he annoys or embarrasses you, you'll still love him, and if you remember that you love him next time they bully you, then you'll stand up for him and stand up to them.'

'What do you know about it, Miss Know-it-all?' shouted Sam. 'You think you're so clever with your big town accent and your big town ways, but you don't know anything.'

As soon as he had said it, Sam was sorry, but Polly

was already folding up the blanket and packing her bag. She made her way to the gap in the hedge without looking back.

'I didn't mean it, Polly,' Sam called after her. 'I'm sorry.'

Polly turned to face him. 'You're not the only one with problems, so don't keep pushing people away when they try to help you, because one day maybe they won't come back.'

A sudden movement on the other side of the hedge made them freeze on the spot. A gruff voice called out, 'Who's there? What are you doing? That's private property. Come on out before I get the police on to you.'

'Run!' yelled Sam. He grabbed Polly's blanket and bag and raced off across the meadow towards the woods. Polly ran after him, but as they reached the edge of the woods, Sam suddenly gasped, 'Our bikes, what about our bikes?'

They looked round. A man had already pushed his way through the hedge. He was standing at the edge of the field wondering whether to give chase, when he spotted the bicycles. Polly and Sam ducked out of sight behind a screen of trees and watched. The man went over to the bicycles, inspected them carefully, then began to push them towards the gap in the hedge.

'He's taking them!' cried Sam.

'Does yours have your name on it?' asked Polly.

'No, but what are we going to do?'

'Wait till he's gone, then start walking I guess.'

'Mum and Dad will go berserk when they find out I've lost it.'

Sam couldn't believe how calm Polly appeared. Not only were they skiving off school, but now they'd lost their bikes as well. 'Aren't you scared someone will find out about us?'

'I'd rather run the risk, than die of boredom.'

Sam tried to shuffle his own fears into some sort of order, and decided that he too would rather run the risk than go back to school and face them.

'Will you write that letter for me?' he asked. 'I'm not ready to go back to school yet.'

'Will you invite me to tea?' replied Polly. 'I'm not ready to go home to Miss Dumpton yet.'

# CHAPTER ELEVEN

By the time they reached home, Sam was full of
anxiety that his parents would notice that he didn't
have his bicycle with him. He was also ravenous.
One cup of tea was all they had had since breakfast.
Luckily, no one was looking out and they managed
to creep up the garden path unseen. Sam opened the
front door.

'Mum,' he called, suddenly feeling very awkward
as well as anxious, 'I've brought a friend back with
me. Is it all right if she stays for tea?'

As Hetty came into the hall, Sam saw a flicker of
annoyance cross her face, but it was gone almost as
soon as it appeared, to be replaced by a look of
curiosity. She held out her hand to welcome Polly.

'This is Polly, from school,' Sam mumbled. 'She's

an evacuee, and she's staying with an old lady in the village.'

'Pleased to meet you, Mrs Lonsdale. I'll go if it's not convenient.'

'Sam's friends are always welcome, but have you ever had chickenpox, Polly? Sam's sister, Clare, is in bed with it and it's extremely infectious.'

'Had it when I was two,' smiled Polly. 'You couldn't see me for spots.'

'You're lucky then. Sam hasn't had it yet, and the older you are the worse it is.'

Sam grimaced. Knowing Clare, she was bound to give it to him.

'What time's tea, Mum,' he said as they went through to the kitchen. 'I'm starving.'

'School dinners not up to much today then?'

'Not enough to keep a fly alive,' jumped in Polly, to Sam's relief. 'In fact, there was a dead fly in mine.'

'Rationing must be hitting harder than I thought,' laughed Hetty. 'We'll eat in fifteen minutes, if you could lay the table.'

Just then, Arthur came in from the garden. 'Ah-ha,' he smiled. 'You've brought me a helper then?'

'This is Sam's friend, Polly. She's come for tea.'

'Pleased to meet you, Mr Lonsdale. Sam's been telling me about your pigeons.'

'Has he now?' He looked quizzically at Sam. 'Nothing but bad, I expect. Sam doesn't like them very much.'

Sam wanted to protest, but instead he found himself saying, 'I'm going to help you with them, Dad.'

His father couldn't disguise his delight. 'That's good to hear, Sam. We'll turn you into a fancier yet.'

'I said I'd help, that's all,' snapped Sam, irritated that his father was showing him up in front of Polly. He dropped the last two knives and forks loudly on to the kitchen table.

'What's a fancier?' asked Polly.

'It's just a special word for someone who breeds pigeons,' Sam's father explained. 'Come on, I'll show you them.'

'Ten minutes,' warned Hetty, 'or the soup will be cold.'

Polly followed Sam's father down the garden path. Sam walked slowly behind them, a little put out by the way his father had so effortlessly buttonholed his

104

friend, but gratified too that Polly didn't seem to find his father's hobby in any way peculiar. Some of the pigeons were strutting around on the roof of the house; others were on top of the loft, wings out-spread, basking in the warmth of the late afternoon sun.

'If you look through the slats on the left there, you'll see a dozen Old Birds doing their bit for the war.'

Polly peered through the slats where Arthur Lonsdale was pointing. A dozen pigeons were dozing in nest-boxes neatly arranged in three tiers of four.

'Three of them are champions, and two might have become champions this year if it weren't for the war. As it is, I'm using them to breed youngsters for the Royal Air Force.'

'What, in case they run out of planes?' tittered Sam, who was trying not to show too much interest. Polly glared at him.

'Pathetic joke, Sam. What do the RAF want them for, Mr Lonsdale?'

'Some of them will go up in planes with the pilots, carried in special boxes. If a pilot is shot down into

105

the sea, he will release his pigeon with a message giving his whereabouts, the pigeon will fly home, and rescuers will be able to find the missing pilot. Others will be dropped by parachute into enemy occupied territory with instructions and a questionnaire for the finders, who will then send them back with information on enemy positions and so on.'

'What happens if the enemy catches them?' asked Sam, intrigued in spite of himself.

'That's the risk we have to take, and it's a big one. They may be found and redeployed or destroyed by the enemy; they may be found by people who are too scared to do anything with them because of the punishment the enemy, or even their own government, might mete out; and they may not be found at all, in which case they might either disappear for good or eventually find their way back home.'

'You're not giving away any of your best birds, are you, Dad?'

'Those I'm not breeding from, yes. They'll be no good to me if we lose the war in Europe. If the Germans invade us, I'll have to destroy them anyway then. At least this way I can feel that I've done something to help.'

'I would never have believed that pigeons could be so important,' said Polly.

'Since history began,' said Arthur. 'Hannibal used them when he crossed the Alps. They were used to pass on the news of Caesar's conquest of Gaul, that's the Roman name for France, and of Wellington's victory at Waterloo. More than 100,000 pigeons served our country in the First World War.'

Why hadn't his father told him all this before, Sam wondered. It might have helped him to understand the fascination. But then Sam remembered that he hadn't exactly gone out of his way to show an interest in his father's hobby; in fact he had been positively antagonistic towards him whenever the subject was mentioned. With good reason, of course, because it still didn't alter the fact that other people thought it was weird.

'How can you just give them up, Dad?' he asked. 'You've spent years building up your loft.'

'What choice do I have?' said his father quietly. Then, briskly, 'Come on, now, our ten minutes is up, and I, for one, do not like cold soup.'

The soup, accompanied by huge chunks of crusty bread, was made from mushrooms Hetty had collected that afternoon from the field behind the house. Polly eyed it suspiciously before dipping just the tip of her spoon into the pale brown liquid and raising it cautiously to her lips. Sam chuckled out loud.

'Polly thinks you're trying to poison her, Mum.'

'No I don't,' retorted Polly. 'I just wondered how you know they're not toadstools.'

'Years of experience,' smiled Hetty. 'It's just a question of learning what the different varieties look like.'

Polly threw caution to the wind, and plunged in. 'Mmmm, it's delicious! At least if I die I'll die smiling! This is the only decent thing I've had to eat since I've been here.'

'It's getting more and more difficult to cook a decent meal,' agreed Hetty. 'There are shortages in sugar, butter, bacon, eggs –'

'Brussels sprouts,' interrupted Sam.

'But there's still plenty of cabbage,' laughed Polly.

'Where is it you're staying, Polly?' asked Hetty.

'With a Miss Dumpton, in the village. She's a bit dotty, but very kind, and I'm very lucky, because some of the kids I know are staying with people who are horrid to them. But I am so bored; there's just nothing to do there. She falls asleep over her crochet at half-past seven, snores loudly for an hour, wakes up, makes us a cup of tea, puts in her rollers, takes out her teeth, and disappears off to bed.'

Sam roared with laughter, but realised suddenly how awful it must be for Polly. She was miles away from her home and her family, in a place where she felt like an outsider because things were done very differently, and where she was bored all day at school, and bored again when she went back to her lodgings in the evening. No wonder she had begun taking herself off during the day.

'Polly could come back here after school, couldn't she? Dad needs more help with the pigeons, don't you, Dad?' asked Sam.

'Steady on,' said his mother. 'We can't just go making arrangements without consulting Polly's guardian. She's responsible for Polly and needs to know where she is and who she's with.' Turning to

Polly she continued, 'Perhaps once or twice a week, Polly, if Miss Dumpton doesn't mind, but I'm concerned too about depriving her of your company. She probably enjoys having someone to talk to and fuss around.'

'That's very kind of you, Mrs Lonsdale,' Polly said quickly, seeing that Sam was about to protest that once or twice wasn't often enough. 'In fact, I'd better be going as soon as we've finished eating, before she begins to worry about where I am. I never go back straight from school, but I'm normally back by five.'

'Did you walk here or cycle?' Arthur Lonsdale spoke for the first time since they had sat down to tea.

'I walked,' said Polly. Sam shifted uncomfortably in his seat.

'Then I'll give you a ride back on the old motorcycle if you like.'

'No, no,' said Polly. 'It's all right. I like walking and it's still sunny outside. Thank you very much for the delicious tea, Mrs Lonsdale.'

'My pleasure. Hope to see you again soon, Polly.'

Sam showed her to the door. 'I'll meet you

tomorrow, if you like, by the old barn just up the road from here,' he whispered. 'Don't forget the letter.'

'I'll write it tonight and post it tomorrow. "Dear Headmaster, I am afraid that Samuel has suffered a nasty turn after eating my homemade mushroom soup. I am wondering if a toadstool slipped in by mistake. Samuel is really rather poorly and could be absent from school for a very long time." Will that do?'

Sam giggled. 'Don't you dare. Just say I've got "influenza", same as you.'

'Aye, aye, sir.' Polly saluted and headed off towards the village.

'That's a spirited young lady if ever I met one,' Arthur smiled as Sam went back into the room.

'She's not happy though, is she?' Hetty joined in.

'What do you mean?' said Sam cautiously.

'Well, she puts a brave face on things, but she's hurting underneath. It must be very hard having to leave your home, family and friends to go and live somewhere and with someone you've never set eyes on before. It's good that you've taken her under your

111

wing, Sam. How did you get to know her? She's older than you, isn't she?'

'We just sort of started talking.'

But he hadn't taken her under his wing, had he? She had taken him under *her* wing. He hadn't really given too much thought to her problems. She seemed fine, so he hadn't bothered to look beyond the surface because his own problems were more important. At least he could make up for it from now on.

# CHAPTER TWELVE

It was hot, impossibly hot. Sam threw off his blankets and lay sweltering in his blacked-out room. His mouth felt dry and itchy. Every time he dozed off he was jolted awake by errant dreams of men shouting, his bike disappearing over a cliff into the sea, pigeons parachuting into the hands of his enemies, his father running from a burning house. When his mother came to wake him up in the morning, Sam felt as though he had not slept at all. His head ached and his limbs lay heavy.

'Time to get up, Sam.' Hetty drew the curtains and brilliant sunlight seared across the room.

Sam screwed his eyes up tight and scratched his head furiously. 'Don't feel too good, Mum.'

'Oh, you'll be all right once you're up and about.

You can't start having time off school now. It'll be the holidays before you know it.' She looked at Sam more closely and sighed. 'On the other hand, though, since you've quite obviously got chickenpox, I don't have any choice but to let you stay home.'

'Stay home?' Sam tried to clear his mind to work out why that idea sowed seeds of panic. Wasn't it good that he had the perfect excuse not to go to school? Wasn't it good that he didn't have to spend the day wandering around trying to fill in the time between supposedly going to school and supposedly coming home again? No more pretence, no more lies, no more forged letters. Letters! Polly! Mum would write a letter. Polly was writing a letter. Two different letters. Two different reasons. One puzzled headmaster. The truth will out!

'Actually, I'm fine, Mum.' Sam jumped out of bed and began to clamber into his school clothes. 'I just felt a bit woozy when I woke up.'

'You're not fine, Sam. You're covered in spots.'

Sam looked in the mirror. There was no denying it. His face was covered with angry red blotches. What's more, he really didn't feel very well at all.

'They won't allow you through the school gates looking like that. Chickenpox is extremely infectious.'

Sam sank back on to his bed. What now? There was nothing he could do to stop the chain of events that would lead to his being found out.

'Stay in bed,' said Hetty, looking at him with some concern, 'and I'll bring you a cold drink. Can you manage something to eat as well?'

'No thanks.'

'Try not to scratch those spots, or they'll leave scars.'

Sam pulled the blankets over him and turned to face the wall. Please don't fuss, Mum. Just leave me alone to think. The only hope he had would be if he could sneak out to meet Polly. Some hope that was though. He would probably be seen even before he had gone through the front door, and then how would he explain himself? Just fancied a walk, Mum. Didn't want to tell you because I knew you'd say no. Sam twisted uncomfortably and scratched hard all across his ribs.

'Don't scratch, Samuel Lonsdale. Mummy says

you'll get nasty scars that will never, ever, ever go away.'

Sam opened one eye. Clare stood in the doorway, holding her teddy and wagging her finger at him.

'Aargh!' jeered Sam. 'It's a horrible spotty monster! Help, Mum, help!'

'You're a horrible spotty monster yourself, so there.'

'I'm not as ugly as you are. You're so ugly, plants shrivel up when you go near them.'

'I'm not ugly. You're just being mean.'

It started as a jibe, but, yes, I'm being mean now, and I'm enjoying it.

'You're so ugly, the sun hides behind a cloud whenever you go in the garden.'

'Shut up, Samuel Lonsdale. I hate you, I hate you!'

'You're so ugly, Dad's pigeons stick their heads under their wings whenever you look in their loft.'

Clare rushed across the room and started pummelling Sam with her fists. 'It's not true!' she screamed, just as Hetty came through the door with a drink.

'Are you two at it again? Why can't you be friends for once?'

'He says I'm ugly. I'm not, am I, Mummy?'

'She shouldn't keep bossing me around then. Bossyboots.'

'That's enough, Sam. You're becoming a bit of a bully towards your sister and I won't have it. Keep your bad temper to yourself.'

Me! Bully! I'm not a bully! I should know! They're bullies, not me! Just because I have a little go at my sister, who deserves it for being so annoying, all of a sudden I'm the bully!

Sam couldn't believe the unjustness of the accusation. 'I'm not a bully,' he shouted. 'I'm not a bully. You always take her side just because I'm older. Why don't you all just leave me alone.'

To his absolute horror and dismay, Sam began to cry, and once he'd started he couldn't stop. He buried his head in the pillow and tried to stifle the sobs that shook his whole being. He felt his mother sit down on the bed beside him and put her arm across his shoulders, but he didn't want instant comfort and pulled away from her. When he lifted his head to gulp for air, then buried it again, he knew that he didn't want to stop crying. Months of pent-up fear and torment and anger burst from his body with each shuddering sob, until at last exhaustion overwhelmed him and he lay there quite still and strangely calm. He felt his mother's weight shift on the bed and heard Clare whisper, 'Is Sammy going to be all right?'

'Let's go away and let him have a good sleep,' Sam heard his mother whisper back. 'I'm sure he'll feel better then.'

He caught the undertone of anxiety in her voice, even as she tried to convince Clare that there was nothing to worry about, and arrows of guilt threatened to pierce his cushion of calm. His mother's hand stroked his hair, the door chafed the floorboards as it was pulled to, and then there was silence.

Sam lay there unable, or was it unwilling, to move. The calm before another storm. His head began to pound as he took in the ramifications of his outburst: the questions that would follow; the truths he might have to tell that would hurt the people he loved and cause no end of trouble for himself; the lies he might have to tell to protect the people he loved, and himself. There were decisions waiting to be made, decisions he couldn't put off any longer. Well, the game was up, wasn't it? Wouldn't it be best to get it all off his chest and let other people deal with it?

No. Not yet. Not now. Sam wished Matt was around. He wouldn't have got into this mess in the first place if Matt had been there. He turned on to his back and scratched savagely at a patch of spots on his forehead, then grimaced wryly to himself: they're biting, Matt, they're biting. But what about you, Matt? Where are you now? What's it like to be in a strange country, far away from us, unable to speak to us, sleeping rough, in danger probably, not knowing when you will be able to come home, nor what you will be coming home to? Sam couldn't even begin to imagine what it would be like, except that he didn't think that he would be brave enough to cope.

He wasn't brave enough. He was letting Matt down. He wasn't strong enough. He was too tired. His legs and arms ached. His head was so full of turmoil it was ready to burst, until finally sleep stole in to provide a welcome refuge.

Voices. His father. Polly? Laughter. Polly? Where was he? Sam struggled to open his eyes. He was in

119

bed in his blacked-out room. He lay there listening to the jumble of sounds which filtered from down below. Polly again. Definitely Polly. Why was she there? What time was it? Sam got out of bed and went to the door to listen. Clattering plates. Wireless. Clare murdering the piano. Polly and his father talking. About what? Sam strained to hear, but could only distinguish the odd dismembered word above the general household hullabaloo and the discordant protestations of the piano. Were they talking about him? He heard the back door open and the voices stretched away.

'Wait for me! I'm coming too!' Sam heard the lid of the piano crash down.

'No you're not, young lady,' his mother's voice rang loud and clear. 'It's too hot and the feathers will aggravate your spots.'

Sam crossed the room and opened his curtains. The sun was shining brightly, but Sam could tell from its position that it was late in the afternoon. How long did I sleep? he wondered. His father and Polly were heading down the garden path to the pigeon-loft. Polly was carrying a bowl of feed, and

Sam felt a pang of resentment that she was taking his place, even though he was aware that just at that moment he had neither the energy nor the desire to do it himself. Then he remembered the letter and a knot of panic tightened in his stomach. Had Polly sent it yet? Perhaps she had come to warn him, because by now she must have realised that his mother would send one as well, may already have sent it. He scrambled into some clothes and made his way downstairs. As he reached the bottom stair, Clare spotted him, ran over and grabbed his hand.

'It's Sammy, Mummy,' she called. 'Are you feeling better, Sammy?' She was trying so hard, and he had been very mean to her. Sam swallowed his irritation and ruffled her hair. 'A bit,' he said gruffly. 'Nice piano playing.'

'I didn't wake you up, did I, Sammy?' Clare put a finger to her lips. 'Don't tell Mummy will you.'

I'm not telling Mummy about a lot of things, thought Sam uneasily. Clare led him into the kitchen, where Hetty was making pastry. 'Sammy's feeling better, Mummy, and he's my friend now, aren't you, Sammy?'

Sam nodded sheepishly, then went over to his mother and leant his forehead against her shoulder. 'Sorry, Mum,' he muttered.

'We all need to let off steam sometimes,' said Hetty, resting her chin on his head. 'Just don't take it out on your sister. Talk to me, Sam. I can't help you if I don't know what's going on.'

'There's nothing, Mum, honest. I just don't feel very well.'

Sam glanced at his mother and saw that she was far from convinced. He changed the subject quickly. 'I heard Polly's voice.'

'She's helping your father. And she brought your bike back.'

'My bike?' Sam couldn't help sounding astonished and his mother looked at him curiously.

'That metal thing with two wheels and pedals that you ride around on.'

'And it's got a seat,' said Clare knowledgeably.

'Very funny, Mum.' Sam recovered his composure. 'I'd forgotten about it, that's all.'

What on earth had Polly said, and how had she managed to get his bike back?

'It was only yesterday that you lent it to her. I'd rather you didn't, Sam. It's kind of you, but there is a war on and we can't afford to be too generous. We might all need our bikes in an emergency.'

Just then, Polly came in from the garden. She looked at Sam and grinned hugely. 'What an improvement! Especially the one on the end of your nose.'

Sam automatically felt the end of his nose. Polly winked at him, and Clare giggled loudly. 'Ha, ha, very funny,' he said, cross that Polly should show him up in front of his sister. Anyway, this was no time for joking. He wanted to know what was going on.

'I'm afraid I can't stay and entertain you.' Polly pulled down the corners of her mouth. 'Miss Dumpton is cooking a rare treat for me tonight: faggots in gravy with pease pudding and dumplings, followed by spotted dick without the spots because she can't get any currants. She says I need fattening up.'

'Well that should certainly do it,' laughed Hetty. 'Polly, on your way home could you possibly post this letter to the school for me?'

Sam stood mouth agape as Polly took the letter from his mother.

'Of course, Mrs Lonsdale. Hope you feel better soon, Sam. We'll start to miss you.'

Polly winked at him again as she walked out into the hall. Sam followed her to the front door and whispered urgently, 'You won't post it will you? Just throw it away somewhere.'

'I'll have to post it,' said Polly, feigning outrage at the suggestion that she shouldn't. 'Your mother has entrusted it to me.'

Sam looked at her aghast. She was supposed to be his friend. How could she do this to him?

'Perhaps I'd better not post my letter though,' Polly smirked. She took an envelope out of her pocket and waved it at him. 'When you didn't turn up today, I thought you might just have chickenpox.' With that, she tore the envelope in half, gave it to Sam, and sauntered off down the road.

# CHAPTER THIRTEEN

Sam felt too unwell to do much over the next few days. He was gripped by intermittent bouts of fever and developed a jarring cough. The spots were unbearably itchy, even though Hetty smothered them painstakingly with a soothing lotion several times a day. The scorching hot weather didn't help, and Sam was happy to let his mother fuss round him while he sat up in bed or in an armchair, the curtains drawn to keep out the sun, reading, playing cards or dozing. When she went to work, his father and Clare looked after him.

Clare, whose own infection was relatively mild, pampered him like a favourite fragile doll – asking him sweetly every five minutes if he was all right, patting him gently on the hand, plumping up his pillow or cushion, straightening his blankets, checking that he had taken his medicine, and asking him over and over again if he thought she would make a good nurse – to the point where he was desperate for her to return to her loud, bossy self.

His father popped in and out from the garden, where he was digging up more of the lawn to make way for his vegetables. Sam thought he looked rather comical in his shorts and heavy boots with his flat cap perched on the back of his head, and sweat pouring down his face. Each time he came in he gave a bulletin on his progress, which was being hampered by the fact that the sun was too hot, the ground too hard, he had blisters on his hands and his back was breaking. But he always went back out again, and Sam couldn't help admiring his determination to get the job done.

Then men from the village started to call on his father. They would disappear into the kitchen together, turn on the wireless, and talk animatedly, sometimes for hours at a time. Sam tried to find out what was going on, but his father was too preoccupied to explain, fobbing him off with 'Not now, Sam' or 'Later, Sam'. Once, when Sam left his chair to answer a knock at the front door, he found the Air Raid Precautions warden from the beach standing on the doorstep. He froze with shock, but the Air Raid Precautions warden simply raised his eyebrows and said, 'Chickenpox, eh? You'll be off school for a while then, no doubt?', then passed on through the hallway to greet his father, leaving Sam red-faced beneath his barrage of purple spots.

At last, after supper one evening, when Clare was in bed and his father was out at a meeting, Hetty sat with him and explained what was happening. 'The Germans have just taken Holland and Belgium, and the Allies seem to be powerless to stop them bulldozing their way across France. If France falls, there is a very real danger that England will be next on Hitler's shopping list.'

'You mean he might attack us?'

Sam tried to make sense of the instant jumble of emotions that made his stomach churn, his skin prickle and his heart pound. There was certainly fear and alarm in bucketloads, but something else. Excitement? Anticipation? Relief? But wasn't this everyone's worst nightmare? Or had the waiting, the not knowing, become a greater nightmare still?

'If France falls, there'll be nothing to stop him invading us,' agreed Hetty.

'Dad says we won't surrender though,' said Sam confidently.

Hetty looked at him and sighed. 'Let's hope we won't ever be in that position, but in any case, the Prime Minister has asked for volunteers to form Local Defence forces around the country. Your father has signed up and they want him to lead our local branch.'

'Like a sort of Dad's army?' chuckled Sam. 'What will they use for weapons? Walking sticks?'

'You may well joke,' Hetty smiled ruefully, 'but that might not be so very far from the truth. Things are going to get very tough, Sam. Once you're better, we'll have to rely on your help to keep things going at home. That includes looking after Clare.'

'Oh no!' cried Sam dramatically, clasping his hands to his chest. 'Anything rather than that. Spare me Clare.'

'Be serious, Sam. Your father and I will be out of

the house a lot and we need to know that you won't be squabbling every five minutes.'

Sam looked at his mother's grave face and nodded. 'I'll do my best, Mum. Don't worry.'

She gave him a hug and he nuzzled his forehead into her neck. The familiarity of her smell was so comforting that he closed his eyes. While part of him was pleased at being treated like an adult and given adult responsibilities, another part wanted only to snuggle up tight like a little boy and have all his cares smoothed away by his mother's gentle caresses. But Hetty sighed and stood up.

'I'd love to sit here and chat for the rest of the evening, Sam, but I've got a stack of paperwork to catch up on. You should get to bed. We need you fighting fit as soon as possible.' Sam noticed that his mother looked rather embarrassed at her choice of expression as she turned away from him.

Things were going to get tough. Weren't they tough enough already? Little did his parents know that he hadn't been able to deal with the minor problems in his own life, let alone take on a major family role with war about to thrust its terrifying reality on to their doorstep.

Suddenly, Sam wanted Polly to be there. Polly, who wasn't scared of anything. Polly, who knew all the answers. Polly, who would help him make sense of the curious cocktail of emotions that was streaming through his body. Where was Polly? She hadn't called by since the weekend and it was Thursday now. He hadn't even had the chance to ask her about his bike. Was she already bored with looking after the pigeons? Or was it, perhaps, that she was bored with him? After all, what could a spotty nearly thirteen-year-old country bumpkin who was too scared even to go to school offer 'the fascinating and mesmerisingly beautiful Pollyanna'? Well, he had shown her her first tractor, hadn't he? Sam smiled wryly to himself at the thought. What an earth-shattering moment that must have been for her!

Just then, Arthur arrived home and walked into the front room carrying a large cardboard box.

'You'll never guess what I've got in here,' he said. Sam couldn't remember his father looking so pleased with himself. Hetty came back into the room and eyed her husband with mock suspicion.

'You look like the cat that's got the cream,' she smiled. 'Open up, then.'

'For someone who's been fighting a rearguard action on behalf of the much-maligned and under-rated pigeon, it might seem like quite a strange thing to have,' said Arthur, 'but in fact it's because of the pigeons that I've been given it.'

'Come on, Dad, what is it?'

'In this box I have something that will propel us on to the front line of modern technology,' said Arthur teasingly.

'If you don't tell us what it is,' replied Hetty, 'I'll propel you to the bottom of the garden and shut the door behind you.'

With great ceremony, Sam's father opened the box and slowly pulled out the contents.

'A telephone!' exclaimed Hetty.

Sam was astonished. He had only ever seen a telephone in his headmaster's office at school. It wasn't the sort of thing anyone he knew would be able to afford. He stared at the black, daffodil-shaped apparatus and wondered how it worked.

'It's only a second-hand one, of course,' said his

father. 'The newer ones are a completely different shape.'

'Can we ring someone?' said Sam, suddenly feeling very excited about this new development in their lives.

'Not until the engineers have been and wired it up,' his father replied.

'But what on earth do we want a telephone for, and who's going to pay for it?' asked Hetty.

Sam realised that his mother was far from delighted with the gadget now sitting on her sideboard, and was worried that his father's moment of triumph would be spoilt, but Arthur waved his hand as though to dismiss any objections.

'It's all right, Het, it's free,' he said. 'I've been given it because people from the National Pigeon Service will need to contact me, as well as the police and local government officials.'

'Well I hope I won't ever have to answer it if it rings,' said Hetty. 'I shouldn't know what to say.'

'That would be most unusual,' said Arthur, winking at Sam and walking out of the room before Hetty had cottoned on to what he meant.

Sam recognised a change in his father. Life was becoming progressively more difficult by the day for them as a family, and especially for his father. He was unable to indulge his passion for pigeon racing and had given away some of his most valuable birds. His work as a master carpenter had virtually dried up, apart from the odd minor repair job. Sam knew from listening to the wireless that supplies of wood and other materials were being diverted towards the war effort, and in any case nobody was likely to be thinking about new dressers and tables at such a time. And then there were the inevitable fears about Matt's safety. Yet his father seemed less remote, more communicative, happier somehow.

'Dad's happy,' Sam said to his mother.

'He's got a new gadget to play with and he feels needed.' Hetty pulled a face at the telephone. 'Now come on, off to bed with you. You've cluttered the place up long enough for one day.'

The telephone rang in the night. Sam ran to answer it. When he picked up the handset a voice whispered, 'Coooeeee, we're coming to get you. You can't escape. We're in your house. We're in your head.'

Sam slammed down the handset, but the telephone rang again. Sam tried to block out the sound, but the ringing went on and on and on. He couldn't bear it. He picked up the handset and screamed into it: 'Leave me alone, why don't you leave me alone!'

A voice whispered, 'Coooeeee, the Germans are coming to get you. You're surrounded. No one can save you now.'

Sam grabbed the telephone and hurled it across the room. 'My father can save me,' he yelled. 'You've got it all wrong. My father will save me!'

Sam woke up soaked in perspiration. He had no idea what time it was, but there were no sounds from anywhere in the house. He closed his eyes again and fell into a deep and easy sleep.

# CHAPTER FOURTEEN

Polly didn't come by again until Saturday morning. Sam was desperate to talk to her, but Clare ran to answer the door before he even knew what was happening. She came back into the kitchen cradling a huge bunch of rhubarb stalks.

'Look, Mummy, Polly brought us some rhubarb. Can we have crumble, please, Mummy, please?'

'It's from Miss Dumpton,' Polly explained as she reached the kitchen doorway. 'She says it's swamping everything in her garden and would I please give some to my friends.'

'Bet it tastes horrid when she cooks it,' grinned Sam.

'It makes your eyes water and your lips pucker,' nodded Polly, pulling a face to demonstrate, which

Clare immediately copied. 'I'm surprised it doesn't knock out her false teeth.'

'Polly!' admonished Hetty with mock severity. 'Miss Dumpton is very kind and I won't have her ridiculed. Anyway, you'll all have to get used to watering eyes and puckered lips because sugar is becoming extremely scarce. Now, if you want crumble, clear out of my kitchen all of you.'

Clare quickly grabbed hold of Polly's hand and pulled her out through the back door.

'Let's go and see the pigeons, Polly. Mummy wouldn't let me till today because of my spots, but they're nearly gone so it's all right now, and Daddy says there are lots of eggs, but Sam's still got spots so he can't go and see them, but he doesn't care because he doesn't like them.'

Sam looked on crossly while an amused Polly allowed herself to be dragged down the garden path.

'She's doing it again, Mum, bossing people around and taking over. Polly's my friend, not Clare's.'

'Polly can look after herself, Sam. Anyway, as soon as they come back in I'll find something for Clare to do and you two can go off for a walk. Some fresh air and sunlight will do those spots good.'

Sam was relieved to be leaving the house after a week of quarantine, and to feel that his strength was returning. He was pleased too to have Polly to himself for a while.

'I thought you'd abandoned us,' he said, hoping not to sound as though it mattered.

'I've been captured, tried and sentenced since I saw you last,' Polly cried dramatically. 'The late night knocking on the door, the interrogation, the breaking of my spirit which bulldozed me into an admission of guilt, and now the lifetime of forced labour which I have no choice but to endure. Oh woe is me!'

'What on earth are you talking about?' Sam didn't know whether to laugh at Polly's histrionics, or to panic in case he too was about to get into trouble over the bike episode.

'School! I've been sent back to school! Woe is me!'

Sam stared at Polly, speechless with confusion.

'Who's sent you back to school?' he finally managed to ask.

'The Billeting Officer. I was spotted by some big-bosomed busybody "committing an indecent act in a public place". She frogmarched me to the police station, who got in touch with the Billeting Officer, who got in touch with Miss Dumpton, who was very dismayed that I had let her down but who wants to keep me as long as I promise to go to school like a good girl.'

'What sort of indecent act?' Sam asked tentatively, afraid of what he might be about to hear.

'I was only having a wee behind a tree,' Polly stated indignantly. 'Not exactly a crime, is it? Anyway, it's not my fault if there aren't any public lavatories in the countryside, and it was her fault for coming along when she did.'

Sam flushed bright red and snorted with laughter.

'There's nothing funny about being caught with your knickers round your ankles, Samuel Lonsdale. I'll have to chase you for that.'

Sam raced off along the road with Polly at his heels. They stopped by a low wall surrounding a large meadow and flopped down on to the grassy verge. For a moment they sat in silence, heads thrown back against the wall, and listened to their gasps for breath gradually dwindling. The only other sound was the occasional twitter of a bird from a hedge further along the road.

'Are you scared?' Polly's sudden question burst through the silence like a gunshot.

Sam frowned. 'What of?'

'The war, you dolt. What do you think I'm talking about? I'm scared. Very scared.'

'I thought you meant scared of going back to school.'

Polly looked at him with contempt. 'Of course I wasn't talking about stupid school. That's just namby-pamby kids' stuff, stuff you can deal with yourself if you make up your mind to. I'm talking about the real world, where everything's spinning out of control. I'm talking about going home and finding there's nothing to go home to because it's all been blown to bits. I want my mum. I miss my mum, and I'm scared that something will happen to her when I'm not there.'

Sam looked on helplessly as Polly burst into angry tears. So this was what his mother had meant when she said that Polly was hurting inside. How would he feel if he was away from home and something happened to his parents so that he would never see them again? Sam thought that he would rather be there beside them, come what may.

He wanted to say something to Polly, to make her believe that everything would be all right. But what could he say? There were no words he could use to reassure her because nothing was certain any more, and Polly knew that as well as he did. The only comfort he could provide was to be there for her.

He stretched out a hand and held her clumsily by the shoulder: it was all the encouragement she needed to turn towards him, bury her face against his chest and howl with anguish.

Sam rested his cheek against the top of her head and held her, then lifted it again when he recalled, fleetingly, the rest of what she had said: something about 'namby-pamby kids' stuff' and 'making up his mind to deal with it'. He pushed it from his thoughts; this wasn't the time to challenge her.

Polly's howl lessened to a sob and then to an intermittent sniff. She pulled away from Sam and blew her nose loudly.

'I've soaked your shirt with my tears,' she declared. 'That means you'll have to marry me. Old English country tradition.'

'Ha, ha,' said Sam, relieved to see the return of the Polly he knew.

'Don't you want me then?' Polly loaded the question with tragic despair.

'Not on your nelly!' replied Sam, and they collapsed with laughter at the ridiculousness of the expression.

Just then, they heard voices from somewhere behind them. They stood up and gazed over the wall. Four men were dragging a rusty old iron bedstead across the coarse grass and into the centre of the meadow.

Polly turned to Sam and shook her head. 'You really do have some very strange customs in the countryside. Are they planning to sleep under the stars?'

''Course not,' sniggered Sam, who hadn't a clue what they were doing. 'They haven't got a mattress.'

One of the men turned round and Sam saw, suddenly, that it was his father.

'Hey, Dad, what are you doing?'

Arthur waved to them and yelled back, 'Preventing Jerry from using this meadow as an airstrip. He won't find a flat piece of ground to land on anywhere in England if we old-timers have our way.'

'Looks more like you're offering him a bed for the night,' joined in Polly.

'He'll find cold comfort here,' laughed Arthur.

The men went off to search for other large pieces of scrap to strew across the fields. Sam and Polly wandered back up the road.

'I feel better for talking to your dad,' Polly said. 'He makes you feel everything's going to be all right because he really seems to believe it himself.'

Sam nodded his head. He felt a tug of pride at Polly's remark, a relief from the shame he had felt for so long.

Almost as though she sensed it, Polly asked, 'What are you going to do, Sam?'

He wasn't sure what she meant.

'About school?' said Polly. 'Your chickenpox will be gone in a few more days, then what?'

Sam didn't answer. This was the question he had

been trying to avoid, even though he knew he couldn't run away for ever.

'I think you should go back. Go back and face up to them.'

Sam still didn't speak. A whirlpool of emotions spun through him so fast that no organised thoughts could find their way through.

Go back? Could he? Face them? Can't. Face them? Don't want to. Why not? Namby-pamby kids' stuff. Deal with it. Not namby-pamby kids' stuff. Scared. Why? Deal with it. Make up your mind.

'They can't hurt you any more, Sam,' Polly insisted.

Yes they can! Bet they can. Namby-pamby kids' stuff. Face them. Scared. Deal with it. Make up your mind.

'Your dad's worth a hundred of them.'

'I know that,' Sam almost shouted. 'Do you think I don't know that?'

'Go back then, Sam. I'll be there to support you.'

'No you won't,' snapped Sam. 'You keep out of it. It's my problem. I'll sort it out myself.'

They walked on in silence again for a few minutes,

then Polly looped her arm through Sam's and said, 'At least you didn't go storming off this time.'

Sam allowed himself a wry smile, then remembered the question that he had been wanting to ask Polly for days.

'How did you get my bike back?'

'Easy,' grinned Polly. 'I saw it leaning against the wall of the police house and when no one was looking I took it. Then I went back and took Miss Dumpton's.'

Sam gazed at Polly aghast. 'What if someone had seen you? Weren't you scared of being caught?'

'Doing what? Taking back our rightful property? No crime in that. That man shouldn't have taken them in the first place.'

We shouldn't have been trespassing in the first place, thought Sam.

Polly seemed to read his mind again because she continued, 'We weren't doing any harm, were we? Anyway, it's not right that someone should keep all that land to themselves.'

'S'pose not,' said Sam, wondering whether as a country boy it might be traitorous to agree with such a view.

They arrived back home to be greeted by the sweetly sour smell of rhubarb crumble filtering through an open window, and a man's sombre voice coming from the wireless.

'Smells good,' said Sam.

'Sounds bad,' said Polly.

In the kitchen, Hetty stood by the wireless listening intently. She waved to Sam and Polly to be quiet as they came in. They heard the newsreader say something about the British Expeditionary Force being pushed back towards the Normandy coast and the fall of France seeming inevitable.

Hetty switched off the wireless, sat down heavily at the table and shielded her eyes with her hand.

'What does it mean, Mrs Lonsdale?' asked Polly.

'It means that the Allies are losing, Polly. If France falls, we're next in the firing line.'

'Yes, but you should see what Dad's doing to stop them landing here, Mum.'

'Mr Lonsdale and his troops are ready for them,' Polly smiled ruefully.

'Let's hope they are,' sighed Hetty. 'But I'm worried about Matt, too. Who knows where he is in France and what danger he might be in.'

'He'll be all right, Mum, you know Matt.' Sam tried to sound convincing as much to convince himself as his mother. He suddenly realised that his role had changed. Here he was trying to protect his mother, whereas not so long ago she had been trying to protect him. 'Come home, Matt,' he begged silently, 'please come home. You're better at this than me.'

'My brother's a prisoner-of-war.' Polly stated this so baldly that for a moment Sam wondered if he had heard correctly.

'Oh, Polly, I'm so sorry.' Hetty sprang to her feet and put an arm round her.

'You didn't tell me that,' said Sam, then wished he hadn't because it sounded rather peevish.

'He sent Mum a letter, about three weeks ago. Said he was being forced to march to a concentration camp with thousands of other POWs. Said they were herded into fields at night like cattle. Said he was so hungry that he would eat his boots if he didn't need them to march in. But Mum thinks he's better off being a prisoner-of-war than fighting. At least he won't get killed then, she says.'

Polly rubbed her nose and Sam thought she was going to burst into tears again, but instead she said, 'Mrs Lonsdale, I think the crumble's burning.'

Hetty rushed to the cooker and opened the door. A cloud of grey smoke billowed across the kitchen. Hetty pulled out the crumble and stared at it in dismay. 'Blast this war!' she cried. 'Look at it. Burnt to a cinder. Just when we can't afford to go throwing things away.'

'Don't throw it away,' said Polly. 'I'm used to burnt. Miss Dumpton's always burning things. Anyway, it's probably all right underneath.'

'Bless you, Polly.' Hetty hugged her gratefully. 'You're so good at looking on the bright side.'

'Not as good as Mr Lonsdale,' grinned Polly.

Later that afternoon, Sam's father arrived home and dug out three wicker baskets from the cupboard under the stairs.

'Time to send some of those youngsters out to earn a living,' he said. 'Can't have them thinking

147

they can just sit around all day preening themselves.'

'Where are they going, Mr Lonsdale?'

'The Air Force wants eight of them, and I'm sending one of my Old Birds to the Intelligence Services.'

'Which one, Dad?'

'The Duke of Wellington.'

Sam was shocked. 'But you said he's the best bird you've ever had.'

'That's why the Intelligence Services want him. So, are you two going to round them up? There's a despatch rider coming to collect them in an hour. It shouldn't do you any harm to go near them now, Sam. In fact, I think you'll be going back to school early next week.'

'How do we know which one is the Duke of Wellington, Mr Lonsdale?'

'He's got a big barrel chest, short legs and pigeon toes. If you can't recognise him from that description –' Sam's father peered out of the kitchen window – 'he's the blue one sitting with his wings outspread on the right-hand edge of the pigeon-loft roof.'

Sam and Polly set off down the garden path with

148

the baskets and a bowl of corn.

'I can't believe Dad's going to let the Duke go. He's had him for four years now and he's won dozens of races.'

'I thought you didn't know anything about your dad's pigeons?'

'You can't help knowing something about someone's obsessions when you live with them,' Sam retorted. He rounded on Polly, remembering her remark from earlier. 'What you said to me – it's not namby-pamby kids' stuff. You shouldn't have said that. It might seem small and pathetic compared to other things, but when you're in the middle of it and it's all the time and it won't go away, it feels huge and it takes over your life. I thought you understood.'

Polly nodded. 'I do understand and I'm sorry, I shouldn't have said what I did. I was just upset with everything. But I do think you're ready to deal with it, Sam.'

'We'll see,' said Sam dismissively, unwilling to think further ahead than he had to. 'Right now, I'm on a mission to catch the Duke of Wellington.'

# CHAPTER FIFTEEN

Sam went back to school on Tuesday. He had no choice. Arthur offered him a lift on his motorcycle, and refused to listen to any arguments.

'I've got to go that way anyway, so we might as well spare your legs, especially in this heat.'

Sam was horrified. What if they saw him? It would all start up again before he had even had time to settle his feet back under his desk. But then he remembered Polly's words, and he realised that, once again, he was sacrificing his feelings for his father to their malicious games. He was proud of his father, wasn't he? He loved his father, didn't he? He wrapped his arms round him and held on tight, so tight that Arthur laughed and said, 'If you hold me any tighter, you'll squeeze my pips out!'

As the motorcycle spluttered along the road, Sam tried to stay resolute. 'You can deal with it,' he said to himself over and over again but, as they approached the village, his emotions began to fluctuate between determination to stand up to their bullying, and fear that he might just make things worse. By the time they reached the school lane, Sam felt sick and wanted to go back home.

'You can drop me here, Dad,' he shouted above the noise of the motorcycle. 'I'll walk the last few yards.'

'Don't want to be seen with me, eh?' Arthur chuckled as he pulled up by the pavement. 'I don't blame you. Can't have your old dad cramping your style.'

'It's not that, Dad,' Sam protested. 'I just need a walk.'

'It is that, Dad,' he said to himself guiltily, 'but not for the reasons you think.' Even when Arthur said goodbye and patted him on the arm, Sam looked round to make sure no one had seen. And then suddenly he found himself asking, 'Dad, were you ever bullied at school?'

Arthur Lonsdale looked quizzically at his son. 'No,

I wasn't,' he answered slowly. 'Why? Is someone bullying you?'

'No, Dad, not me. A friend of mine.'

Tell him, Sam. Tell him. You're halfway there. Tell him.

'A friend of mine was bullied once,' said Arthur.

'How did he deal with it?' Sam tried not to sound too desperate to know.

'He began to believe in himself: in who he was and what he thought and what he felt and what he stood for. And when he realised that he was happy with himself, he knew that nobody could hurt him any more, whatever they might say or do.'

Sam stood for a moment, taking in his father's words and nodded his head. 'I'd better go, Dad. I'll be late.'

Arthur slid off the motorcycle and put his arm round his shoulder. 'Have a good day, Sam. I hope your friend can believe in himself enough to deal with those bullies.'

Sam freed himself from his father's grasp, but just as he began to walk away, he heard, 'Morning, Mr Lonsdale.'

He turned to see one of them greeting his father.

'Morning, Tim,' said Arthur. 'I'll be over to see your father this evening.'

'I'll let him know, Mr Lonsdale. Morning, Sam. Glad to see you back.'

I bet you are! I bet you are! Sam scowled, nodded his head abruptly, and the boy smirked at him before continuing along the lane, whistling loudly .

'That's Roger Baldwin's son. Nice lad.' Arthur climbed back on to his motorcycle and started up the engine. As he drove away, he shouted, 'Roger's one of my local defence volunteers.'

The groundswell of anger that had boiled up inside Sam as soon as this boy had addressed his father threatened to erupt uncontrollably. He wanted to smash his face in for daring to go near his father after everything he had done. He wanted to wipe that smirk off his face once and for all. Nice lad, eh? The three of them had pushed him through a whole gamut of emotions, but never had Sam felt anger like this before. This was anger that vanquished every trace of fear. If they wanted war, they could have it.

Sam sprinted along the lane. He was too late, though. The boy had already disappeared amongst the crowd of children who were jostling their way through the school gates. Sam kicked the railings in frustration, then leant against them and tried to calm himself down. He was ready, he knew it. He just had to be patient and wait for the right moment.

Sam had only been away from school for two weeks, but when he passed through the school gates it seemed more like two months. He felt like a total stranger and almost expected to be treated as such. But when he walked across the playground, he was quickly swallowed up by a group of friends who appeared genuinely delighted to have him back. Demands for the intimate, gory details about his spots were interspersed with gossip and grumbles about teachers and 'you-wouldn't-believe-this' stories about 'those ignorant vacks'.

Sam didn't see Polly, though he scoured the playground for her, and they weren't around either. He was able to enjoy being the centre of attention, at least for a brief moment.

Nothing happened that day, of course. Sam wasn't

really surprised. They dictated the terms, and they seemed to delight in playing the waiting game. Some malevolent sense told them that it made things worse for their victim. It certainly did for Sam now, because he wanted something to happen, and he didn't know whether he could hold out if they made him wait too long. They were stealing his thunder.

Polly waved to him at lunchtime, but she didn't seem too interested in spending any time with him, and why should she? he reasoned, she was in a higher year, after all. So he settled down to his lessons and tried to rebuild relationships with his classmates.

At home that evening, after they had finished supper and Arthur had gone out to meet up with his local defence volunteers, Hetty switched on the wireless to listen to the news. From the newsreader's voice, it immediately became clear that the news was not good. He reported in sombre tones that many thousands of British and French troops were stranded on the beaches of the Normandy port of Dunkirk.

While Clare, oblivious, clunked away on the piano, Sam sat down with his mother and they listened with increasing disquiet. The newsreader described how the Allies had been forced to retreat, until they were surrounded by the Germans on one side and the sea on the other. Now, they were being subjected to a barrage of aerial attacks, and there was nowhere for them to shelter.

All the time, more and more exhausted troops were arriving on the beaches, only to find that they too were trapped. Their only hope of survival was to be evacuated, and soon, but there weren't enough ships in the area to cope with the sheer numbers.

A loud, persistent ringing broke into the broadcast and punctuated Clare's piano playing. Nobody moved. Sam looked at his mother, and Hetty looked back at him.

'What's that noise, Mummy?' Clare looked anxious and tried to sit herself on Hetty's lap, but Hetty suddenly jumped to her feet and, after a moment's further hesitation, picked up the telephone handset and spoke into it very precisely.

'Hello. This is Mrs Hetty Lonsdale. Who is calling, please?'

'Why is Mummy talking to that black thing?'

Clare was wide-eyed with astonishment.

'It's your father,' Hetty whispered to Sam.

Clare giggled. 'That's not Daddy. Mummy's being silly, isn't she, Sammy?'

'Shhh,' said Sam, trying to hear what his mother was saying.

There was silence as Hetty listened intently, then she said, 'But you're not to go yourself, Arthur. Promise you won't go yourself.'

More silence, then, 'Well, I'll see you sometime tomorrow. Wish everyone a safe journey, and, don't worry, Sam and I will make sure the pigeons are fed.'

Hetty carefully replaced the handset and looked at Sam. Clare darted across the room and demanded to be lifted up.

'Silly Mummy,' she giggled again. 'Why were you pretending that black thing was Daddy?'

'It's called a telephone, poppet, and I can hear Daddy's voice through it. Come on, up to bed with you, and I'll try to explain.'

As they left the room and went up the stairs, Sam could hear Clare demanding to know where her father was and why his voice was in the black thing.

Where was he, Sam wondered too, and why wasn't he coming home that night? Sam couldn't remember his father ever having stayed away overnight. And what was his mother talking about when she made him promise not to go himself? When at last she came back downstairs, Sam was shocked to see how tired and anxious she looked.

'What's going on, Mum?' he asked as she collapsed into a chair.

'Two of the local defence volunteers have fishing boats which operate off the south coast. They want to sail them over to Dunkirk to help bring out some of the soldiers. Have you ever heard anything so foolish? The Channel's full of mines and submarines, and I should think the last thing the Navy wants is a whole load of little boats getting in its way. Anyway, your dad's gone down to the coast to help empty the fishing boats of nets and tackle and load them up with food and medical supplies.'

'Dad's not going over there himself, is he?' Sam was alarmed.

'He says not, but I don't know, Sam. Will he be able just to stand by and watch?'

Sam doubted it, not from what he'd learned about his father in recent weeks.

'He doesn't know anything about sailing though, does he? He'll be back tomorrow, Mum, I'm sure he will.'

'I hope so, Sam. It's bad enough not knowing where Matt is. I don't think I could cope with your father disappearing as well.'

Sam suddenly felt cross with his father for putting his mother through so much worry; for leaving him to deal with this as well as with everything else.

'Has Mr Baldwin gone with them?'

'I believe so. It was his house Arthur was telephoning from. Why do you ask?'

How strange that fate should keep throwing the fathers together when the sons are at war.

'Dad said he was going there this evening. Mr Baldwin's son goes to my school.'

'Then he'll be worried about his father too.'

'I bet that won't stop him though, Mum,' thought Sam wryly.

'You'd better get to bed, Sam. We'll have to be up early in the morning.'

Sam gave Hetty a big hug. 'Don't worry, Mum. Dad won't do anything stupid.'

'Brave is sometimes stupid,' said Hetty quietly, 'and your father's one of the bravest people I know.'

# CHAPTER SIXTEEN

Sam woke at five o'clock and couldn't go back to sleep. He pulled open the blackout and let in the most glorious May morning. What he missed by sleeping so late every day! The sky sparkled blue and the air was filled with the eager twitter of breakfasting birds. Somewhere close by, a nest of fledglings clamoured for food. A neighbour's cat strolled nonchalantly across what little was left of the lawn. Sam banged on the window to frighten it away, in case it harboured plans to squat amongst his father's vegetables.

Where are you, Dad? I'll hold the fort for you today, but what happens tomorrow?

Sam dressed, went quietly downstairs and out into the garden. It was already warm. Although he was sure that his father would have watered it the day before, the soil looked dry round the impressive rows of lettuces, beans, peas and other less easily identified vegetables. Sam turned on the hose, squeezed the end to form a spray, and squirted it in swashbuckling fashion from side to side, back and forth, until the soil had turned muddy brown and the leaves glistened with drops of moisture. Then he bent down and checked beneath the leaves for marauding snails and slugs, hurling any that he found into the field beyond the garden fence.

Sam knew that Arthur kept to a strict regime where his pigeons were concerned, and that it was too early to feed them or let them out. But he went to the shed and measured some maize into several clean troughs, then mixed some glucose with water and poured it into a feeding bottle. While he was there, Sam found an identification guide to the pigeons, each bird neatly catalogued with, under its name, drawings showing particular colours and markings, and notes giving details of age, lineage, races entered and prizes won.

He sat down on a wooden box and studied each

bird in turn, surprised by all the variations of eye and neck colour and the different wing markings. If he could learn to recognise them and call them by name, he thought how astonished his father would be, and the idea made him smile to himself. He sat there for some minutes more, flicking backwards and forwards through the meticulous pages of Arthur's guide, then sprang back into action, tidying up the garden tools and wiping the mud from his father's wellington boots.

Satisfied that he had done everything he could for the time being, Sam went back into the kitchen, put on the kettle and cut himself a hunk of bread.

'You woke me up, Samuel Lonsdale.'

Peace shattered.

'I thought you were my daddy.'

Clare stood in the doorway, teddy in one hand, blanket in the other.

'Dad will be back later,' said Sam, trying not to sound grumpy.

'I want him now,' insisted Clare. 'Daddy always lets me help him in the morning.'

'He had something very important to do,' said

Sam, 'so I'm looking after things here for him. If you like, you can help me feed the pigeons.'

'Daddy always pours me some milk first,' Clare informed him, as the whistle from the kettle began to shriek.

Sam duly poured some milk into a glass and plonked it down in front of her.

'And he makes me a piece of bread and jam.'

Sam cut a piece of bread, dropped a large dollop of jam on to it and pushed it across the table to his sister.

'Anything else, Madam?'

The shriek of the kettle reached boiling point.

'You didn't cut the bread straight. I don't like it when the crust's all thick.'

'Then do it yourself next time, fusspot.'

Sam took the kettle off the stove and stormed out of the kitchen into the garden. The day had started so well, yet within minutes his sister had ruined everything. He picked up a fork and rammed it into the ground, then he bent down and pulled savagely at a clump of weeds. They refused to budge, and as he pulled harder he felt his anger turn to fierce determination. He pulled with all his might until, at last, the roots surrendered their hold, and he fell backwards in a heap, the weeds still clutched in his hand.

'Why are you rolling on the ground, silly Samuel?'

Before he had time to answer, Clare's plump, giggling body was on top of him and she was trying to tickle him under his armpits. Sam let her think she had the better of him, then he suddenly grabbed her round the waist and scrambled to his feet. 'You've had it now, my little chocolatey Clare,' he chortled. 'I'm going to throw you in the wheelbarrow.'

'Oh no you're not,' squealed Clare.

'Oh yes I am!'

Sam galloped with her under his arm round the vegetable patch to where the wheelbarrow was standing, lowered her into it, then picked up the handles and began to push her round in circles. Clare screeched with laughter, until, exhausted, Sam tipped her out on to the lawn and dropped to his knees himself.

Clare tried to pull him to his feet. 'More, Sammy, more!'

'No more,' Sam shook his head. 'Let's take Mum breakfast in bed, then we'll feed the pigeons.'

This was better. This was how the day was supposed to go. Sam boiled two eggs and cut a piece of bread into soldiers, while Clare carefully laid a tray. Then he sent her back into the garden to pick a single flower, while he poured tea into his mother's favourite cup. As Sam made his way slowly upstairs, Clare charged ahead and straight into her parents' bedroom. She leapt on to the bed and bounced up and down.

'We've brought you breakfast in bed, Mummy!' she cried triumphantly, before slipping under the blankets and snuggling up to her mother.

The stunned look on Hetty's face was replaced by a broad smile as she sat herself up against the pillows and took the tray from Sam.

'Well, this is a nice surprise. Thank you, Clare. Thank you, Sam.'

'At your service, Ma'am,' said Sam. 'And now, if that's all you require, I must be off to feed the pigeons.'

He saluted and headed off downstairs, but Clare

stayed with her mother, chattering and scrounging soldiers.

How am I doing, Dad? How are you doing, Dad? Are you on your way back yet? I need you to be here tonight. I need you to be here when I come back from school. Don't let me down.

Sam unlocked the loft and went inside. He was greeted by a blast of musty air and turned straight-away to open the vents. The pigeons cooed and bur-bled round his feet and from their perches, their eyes bright, their movements perky. There was some-thing oddly soothing about them, something that inspired calm. Sam took one from its box, and gently stroked its feathers and tweaked its throat as he had seen his father do. 'Hello, Mellow Yellow,' he said. Then he opened one of its wings and studied the neat rows of feathers with their subtly iridescent colours. The pigeon seemed quite happy with this attention, and Sam began to understand his father's obsession.

'Haven't you fed them yet, Samuel Lonsdale? Mummy says it's nearly time for school.'

Clare broke into his thoughts again. Sam put the

pigeon back and took his sister with him to collect the fresh troughs of food from the shed. Before leaving the loft, he opened the traps so that the pigeons could go out.

'Thank you, Samuel.' Hetty nodded her appreciation as Sam dashed upstairs to change into his school uniform. 'Your father would be proud of you.'

'And me, Mummy.' Clare wasn't going to be left out.

When Sam reappeared he hugged his mother goodbye. 'See you later, Mum. Don't worry about Dad. He'll be back today.'

He jumped on to his bicycle, waved to his mother and sister, and set off down the road ahead of them.

# CHAPTER SEVENTEEN

School. Them. Will it be today? I'm ready. I'm ready for you, Peter Simpkins. I'm ready for you, Arnold Tupper. I'm ready for you, Timothy Baldwin. How are you feeling this morning, Timothy Baldwin? Are you worried too? After all, we're in the same boat. Sam grimaced at the inappropriateness of the expression, for it could just be that his father and Timothy Baldwin's father were literally in the same boat, on their way to Dunkirk.

He arrived at school at the same time as Polly and, much to his surprise, she locked her arm purposefully through his and walked in with him.

'Save me from this dreadful place,' she pleaded, wiping her hand across her brow. 'Come to me at midnight on your white charger and take me away, oh handsome prince.'

'You're potty,' Sam laughed self-consciously.

'No I'm not, I'm Polly,' she remonstrated, to groans from Sam. 'So, you won't save me, then?'

'You could come for tea instead.'

'Now that's too good an offer to refuse. And I might be able to persuade Mr Lonsdale to saddle up his charger while I'm there.'

Sam was about to mention his father's absence, when the bell rang.

'Got to go,' cried Polly. 'Don't want to miss any of my lessons.'

She tweaked Sam mischievously on the cheek and disappeared across the playground. It was only then that Sam realised that he had unwittingly put off his confrontation with them for another day. They wouldn't accost him if he was with Polly. He didn't know whether to be pleased or annoyed.

At the end of the day, Sam waited for Polly outside the school gates. He watched as the other children pushed and shoved and ran and strolled past, but there was no sign of Polly. They went by and looked at him curiously, but said nothing. Sam carried on waiting until he was sure that no one else could be left inside, then began to cycle slowly along the road. Polly must have come out before him and gone home to tell Miss Dumpton that she was invited for tea. Sam wondered what Miss Dumpton was really like, and whether her cooking was as bad as Polly made out. He began to speed up then, when he remembered that he would be seeing his father again when he got home.

'Coo-ee!'

The front wheel of Sam's bicycle wobbled. Had he heard right? Was this it?

'Coo-ee! We can see you! How's our little lovebird then?'

Sam's heart hammered against his chest wall, but he stopped pedalling and came to a halt. Where were they? He scanned the churchyard. A snigger? From behind the gravestones?

'Have you pecked her yet, you perverted little vacky-lover?'

So they had seen him with Polly. Typical that they should be amongst the minority who were still trying to stir up trouble between the villagers and the evacuees. Sam was determined not to let them get at him through Polly. He took a deep breath.

'Come out, then, so I can see you,' he called. 'Or are you too scared?'

Silence. Sam imagined them trying to make sense of this change of reaction.

A loud snigger, but no sign of them, and then: 'How's your pigeonpox?'

Very funny, ha, ha.

'Nasty disease, pigeonpox.'

'I survived. Thanks for your concern.'

Silence again. This time, they stood up from behind the gravestones and moved closer together. Strength in numbers.

'Are you trying to be clever?'

'No. I'm just answering your questions.'

Sam's nerves were raw, but he was determined not to let them see.

'How's your father, Timothy?'

Sam registered the look of shock on his enemy's face. Ha! He wasn't expecting that. Got him.

'You leave my father out of it, you poxy pigeon freak.'

'I *was* poxy, but I'm not now, and it's pigeon

fancier, not pigeon freak.'

Sam was actually beginning to enjoy himself. It was all words, only words. He liked words. He played with words. Now that he had come to terms with everything, the words they used had lost the power to hurt him. They could say what they liked, and it was water off a duck's back. Water off a pigeon's back!

'Do you think your father's gone to Dunkirk with my father, Timothy?'

Sam watched the other two boys turn their attention to their crony.

'I said leave my father out of it, weirdo.'

'Sorry. It's just that, since my dad was at your house last night, with them being such good friends, I thought you might know more than me.'

'You're asking for a punch, you stinking creep.'

Violence? That was new. Sam wasn't sure he was prepared for anything physical. His heart began to thump again, but he couldn't be seen to be weakening now.

'I'd better be going then. Can't keep those pigeons waiting.'

Sam started to pedal away. They ran to the church wall and hurled abuse at him, but it was muted compared to what he had had to suffer before. In fact it was all a bit of an anti-climax. Sam had expected more, especially since they had latched on to his friendship with Polly. But perhaps they'd had enough of it, too. Perhaps they were relieved that he had fought back and taken the initiative from them. After all, it must have become pretty boring even for them. Nevertheless, he was so thrilled that he had at last managed to stand up to them, that, as soon as he was out of sight, he wove backwards and forwards across the road and, every so often, lifted his arms and legs in the air and shouted, 'I did it!'

Sam couldn't wait to see his father. Even though he couldn't tell him what he had done and what had happened, he just wanted to be close to him so that his father would know that the rift had finally been healed for good. As soon as he reached home, he pushed through the front gate, dropped his bicycle on the ground and dashed into the house.

'Mum,' he called. 'Is Dad back?'

There was no reply. He searched the rooms but

there was no one in. He went into the garden, but there was no one there either. The pigeons were still out, strutting and cooing on the roof of the loft. The wheelbarrow was still on its side on the grass, where he had tipped Clare that morning. Everything was as he had left it before setting off for school.

Where was everyone? Couldn't they at least have left him a note? You're supposed to be here, Dad. I wanted you to be here. Sam wondered whether to wait or to go out and look for them. He grabbed an apple and sat down irritably on the back doorstep.

'Sam?' A voice broke into his thoughts. 'Are you there, Sam?'

Polly. Yippee! Sam jumped to his feet as she came into the kitchen.

'The front door was open, and since you didn't answer –'

'I did it, Polly, I did it! I stood up to them and they melted away like jelly in the sun.'

'Good for you, Sam.'

She didn't even look at him. She didn't even sound impressed. This wasn't right. This wasn't the great big enormous pat on the back that Sam wanted from

Polly, expected from Polly. After all, she was the only one who could pat him on the back.

'I'm going home, Sam.'

'Going home? You've only just got here. I thought you were staying for tea.'

'I mean back to my real home.'

'But –' Sam struggled to gather his thoughts quickly enough. 'The war. It's dangerous in the towns. That's why you came here.'

'I want to be with Mum. She needs me.'

Sam looked at Polly properly for the first time, and was shocked to see how pale and drawn she was.

'She got a telegram, and someone told the school. My brother was shot trying to escape from the camp. He couldn't stand being cooped up. I knew he'd try to escape, but I didn't think –' Polly gulped for air and a deep shudder racked her body.

'Is he – ?' Sam couldn't say the word. It was too unreal. Or was it that it was too real?

Polly nodded brusquely. 'I'd better go. Got a train to catch. I just wanted to say goodbye.' She gave Sam a quick peck on the cheek and turned to leave.

'Will you write?' Sam couldn't believe that she

could just disappear for good.

'I doubt it. Not much point really, is there? We're never likely to see each other again.' Polly's tone softened then. 'But I'm glad I met you, Sam, and I'm really pleased that you sorted those creeps out.'

Without looking back, she strode quickly down the hall and out through the door, closing it softly behind her.

The silence in the house was unbearable then. Sam felt totally abandoned. He went out into the garden, where at least the pigeons provided him with some sense of stability, albeit irrational. He lay down on the ground and gazed up at the clear, blue sky. It was such a beautiful summer, yet it was passing by almost unnoticed in the atmosphere of foreboding that pre-vailed. Sam had hated the waiting game of war that had been played out over the past few months, but now that it was beginning to explode into reality all around him, a wave of terror overcame him. Polly's brother was dead; shot dead escaping from a pris-oner-of-war camp. Nothing could be more real than that. The war had sucked Polly up into its hideous entrails and would spit her out poisoned by grief and despair. Poor Polly. What was she going home to? No father, no brother, a man she detested, a mother in tears and the imminent danger of bombs on her doorstep. At least she would be with her mother now, and that's what she wanted. But who would be the next victim? Matt? Where was Matt? Where was his father?

The loud and persistent ringing of a bicycle bell made Sam jump to his feet, and Clare's shrill voice cut through the silence of the house.

'Daddy! Daddy, where are you?'

She ran into the kitchen, just as Sam came in from the garden.

'Where's my daddy?' she demanded. 'We've picked heaps and heaps of wild strawberries, and I want to show him.'

She pushed past Sam and out through the back door. Hetty came into the kitchen and Sam saw the anxiety in her eyes.

'Not here then?' she said.

'I hoped he was with you.'

'I thought the longer I stayed out with Clare, the more chance there would be that he might be here

178

when we got back. She's been going on and on and on about him.'

Clare charged in again and threw her arms round Hetty's legs.

'He's not here, Mummy. You said he'd be here and he's not. Why isn't he here? Why isn't he here?'

Clare's tantrum was close to tears and Sam could see that his mother had run out of reassurances. He took hold of the basket of strawberries and patted his sister on the shoulder.

'Hey, Clare,' he said. 'Why don't we take all the stalks off these strawberries so that they're ready to eat, and we'll run up to the farm and ask Mrs Humphreys if she's got any cream. Then we'll go and feed the pigeons and put them away for the night. When Dad comes home, all he'll have to do is put up his feet and eat his strawberries, which will be a real treat for him.'

Clare hesitated for a moment, then grabbed the basket of strawberries, got out a bowl and began to de-stalk them.

'Daddy won't mind if we have some too, will he?' she said, popping one into her mouth. Hetty looked gratefully at Sam.

'Of course not,' he said. 'We've got to test them to make sure they're ripe enough.' He put one in his mouth as well.

They prepared the strawberries and fetched a jug of cream from the farm, while Hetty picked lettuces, tomatoes, carrots, radishes and herbs from the garden to make a salad.

'Your father's certainly been busy out there,' she said as she cut a loaf of bread into large hunks.

When tea was ready, there was still no sign of Arthur. They sat down cheerlessly to eat, but Sam found that he had no appetite and even Clare was quiet. She was holding her teddy and her blanket, and her thumb kept straying into her mouth. Before long her eyes began to close. Hetty gently carried her up to bed, while Sam fed the pigeons and closed them up in their loft for the night.

He came back in to find his mother listening earnestly to the wireless. He sat down beside her and looped his arm through hers.

'Your father's gone, hasn't he?' she said, almost accusingly. 'He would have been back by now otherwise.'

Sam didn't know what to say, but once more he suddenly felt furious with his father for putting them through so much pain. Didn't he care about them? It was that question again, and Sam knew the answer, but right now he found it difficult to believe that his father could just go off like that.

'They say that thousands of soldiers have been rescued. But thousands more are still stranded on the beaches, with the bodies of their friends scattered all around them. How must that feel?'

Hetty sounded so despairing that Sam wrapped his arm round her and she nestled her head into his shoulder.

'They're stood there on the beaches, Sam, and there's nowhere for them to hide, and the bombs are still dropping. And they're dropping on the rescue boats as well.'

I know what you're thinking, Mum. Don't think it. Don't.

'Why, Sam? Why couldn't he leave it to other people this time? He's done his bit. Let someone else play the hero.'

You're the one who talked about the thousands

still stranded amid the bodies and the dropping bombs, Mum. There's your answer.

'Maybe he had no choice, Mum.'

His father was who he was. He didn't do things by halves. If he reached the coast, would he have been able to stand there and watch other people taking boats out? Sam thought not. And how would he have felt about his father if he hadn't gone?

'Anyway, we still don't know that he's gone. He could be helping this side. His motorcycle might have broken down.'

Not very convincing, but possible.

'We've got that telephone thing,' said Hetty. 'He would have rung, wouldn't he?'

'He'll be all right, Mum. I know he'll be all right.'

I've got to believe that, and so have you.

Hetty got to her feet. 'I'm sorry, Sam. I shouldn't be burdening you with all this. Your father and I promised ourselves that we would keep the war away from you and Clare as much as possible.'

'I don't think it's in your hands any more, Mum. There are some things you can't protect me from.'

Sam lay awake in bed that night listening for the

key to turn in the front door, listening for the telephone to ring, listening for any sign that his father was back. And then he saw him, in a tiny fishing boat spilling over with soldiers while bombs dropped all around. Suddenly, from overhead, a cloud of pigeons plunged down towards the boat and lifted him out. They carried him back across the sea, until they hovered above his garden and lowered him gently to the ground. Sam woke convinced that he would go downstairs to find Arthur sitting in his favourite chair in the kitchen, drinking a cup of tea. But the kitchen was empty, the only sound the kitchen clock ticking away the seconds, minutes, hours of his absence.

# CHAPTER EIGHTEEN

Going to school was harder than ever. Sam wanted to stay at home, to be there when his father returned. Once again, he was in the position of having to carry on as though everything was normal.

Three days went by, but there was still no news of Arthur. Word started to leak out that he was missing, along with Timothy Baldwin's father, and Sam began to be plagued by other people's concern. They meant well, he understood that, but there were only so many times he could answer the questions 'Have you heard from your father yet?' or 'Is your father back yet?', and there were only so many times he could listen to the placatory 'Don't worry, he'll be back soon', without wanting to tear his hair out. Worse, people kept lumping him together with Timothy

Baldwin, suggesting that because the two of them had this crisis in common, they could at least support each other. No thank you. No thank you!

And then, when a week had gone by, Sam left school to find himself confronted by Timothy Baldwin, who was propped up against the churchyard wall, his feet sticking out across the pavement. Sam wondered where his cronies were hiding. After all, they only ever hunted in packs. He steeled himself for more trouble.

'Your dad not back yet, then?'

The boy didn't look at him but, seemed to be asking his feet the question.

'No,' Sam replied. 'He's not back.'

'Nor mine. You worried?'

'Who wouldn't be?'

'Do you think they went over?'

'Looks like it.'

'My mum's doing her nut. Thinks he's never coming back.'

Sam didn't know what to say. He didn't really want to share confidences with his enemy.

'Why did they have to go? Tell me that. Why did

185

they have to go? Why couldn't they just leave it to people who're trained for that sort of thing? Anyway, Dad knew his boat wasn't seaworthy.'

Sam pricked up his ears. What was that? Not seaworthy?

'Takes in water like a colander. Don't know how he thought it could make it to Dunkirk, let alone come back with it stuffed to the brim with troops.'

Brave is sometimes stupid. Stupid is stupid.

'Do you mean it would have been a waste of time even trying? Do you mean they were putting their lives at risk for nothing?'

Do you mean your dad was putting my dad's life at risk for nothing?

Sam's enemy shifted uncomfortably, then back-tracked quickly and said savagely, 'Look, we don't even know that they went yet, and we don't know that they took my father's boat, and anyway, I don't even know why I'm talking to you.'

'It's probably because I'm the only one who under-stands what you're going through,' retorted Sam, 'but that doesn't mean I want to talk to you either.'

He clambered back on his bicycle and set off

home. 'Takes in water like a colander.' Was that what had happened?

The news all that week was a mixture of jubilant and desperate. Thousands of troops were evacuated by the Navy from Dunkirk, thousands more died on the beaches while they waited to be saved, or drowned in the sea when their rescue boats were bombed. Others made it back across the Channel, against all odds, in paddle steamers, tugboats and tiny pleasure yachts. Some survived the evacuation only to die from their wounds in hospital before their families could reach them.

Sam stubbornly refused to believe that his father would not come back, even when Hetty seemed to be giving up hope. Morning and evening, he threw himself into carrying out all the jobs his father would normally have undertaken. When he sat down with his mother after Clare had gone to bed, he talked about all the things he would do with his father when he came back, and all the things they would do as a family, especially when Matt was home as well.

And one evening, Sam told his mother about the bullying he had suffered at school, how he had blamed his father, and how he had to believe that his father would come back because he needed him to know that everything was all right between them now. Hetty was appalled at what Sam had had to put up with, and distressed that he hadn't felt able to tell them.

'How could I, Mum?' Sam protested. 'How could I do that to Dad?'

'He's big enough and ugly enough to cope,' said Hetty. 'You're just a child and no one should be allowed to put you through that sort of pain.' And then she added, 'We thought it was the war that was getting to you.'

'A different sort of war,' Sam grimaced.

Another week went by. Even Sam began to find it difficult to stay optimistic, to keep things going. The days drifted past in a fog of apprehension, with school providing a cocoon in which he could escape temporarily his adopted role as family support, and where a shroud of sympathy protected him from the normal demands made of pupils. The evenings lapsed into long silences as the words of reassurance died on his lips. Tears were never far away from his mother's eyes, and harrowing dreams ploughed mercilessly through his sleep.

And then, late one afternoon, there was a knock on the door. Sam opened it to find a man who looked vaguely familiar standing awkwardly on the doorstep.

'Hello, lad. Is your mother in?'

'She's working late at the hospital.'

'I see.'

The man shifted uncomfortably, and Sam wondered whether he should just shut the door on him.

'I came about your father, to say how sorry I am. He's a brave man, your father, very brave,' the man blurted out.

Sam nodded his head.

'We got to Dunkirk and picked up some soldiers, but the boat started to go down as we headed back. Everyone panicked, tried to get away. Most of us made it to another boat, but your father, well, nobody knows what happened to him. All we could do was hope he made it to a different boat, but when I arrived home yesterday morning and heard that he wasn't home yet ... I just came to tell your mother

189

I'm sorry. Look, it's pandemonium down on the coast. Total chaos. The hospitals and railways can't cope with the number of people. There's still a good chance your father will turn up, so don't give up on him.'

Sam glared at the man, anger torching through his body like a laser.

'I'll never give up on him, never,' he snarled.

The man gazed at him in bewilderment and turned to go.

'Will you tell your mother Roger Baldwin called?'

Sam didn't answer. He slammed the door and let the hot tears of rage and anguish pour down his face. How dare that man come to their door when it was all his fault? How dare he tell only half the story? How dare he stand there in the place of their father?

Thank goodness, Sam thought, that his mother was out and Clare was with Mrs Humphreys. He decided there and then not to tell her about Roger Baldwin's visit, not yet anyway. He felt sure that she would give up hope altogether if she heard what had happened.

# CHAPTER NINETEEN

Four days later, the telephone rang early in the morning and wrenched Sam from his sleep. He sat rubbing his eyes, trying to identify the sound, then leapt out of bed and bumped into his mother on the landing as she came out of her own room.

'Quick, Mum. It's Dad, I know it's Dad.'

Hetty gazed at him disquietedly, then hurried downstairs. Sam followed and watched as she hesitated before picking up the telephone and took a deep breath.

'This is Mrs Hetty Lonsdale speaking. Who is calling, please?'

There was a long silence while Hetty listened, giving nothing away as to the identity of the caller, but Sam could tell it wasn't his father and his heart sank.

He studied his mother's grave features and wondered what awful news she might be hearing. At last she said, 'Thank you very much for letting me know. I'll make arrangements to come straight away', and replaced the telephone on the dresser. For a moment she just stood there, staring into space.

'What is it, Mum?' Sam hardly dared ask the question. 'Was it something about Dad?'

Hetty nodded her head and tears began to roll down her cheeks, but she was smiling as well, then laughing and crying all at the same time. She clutched Sam to her and burbled, 'He's alive, Sam. He's in hospital, but he's going to be all right and he sends us his love.'

Sam was laughing too now, and the commotion woke Clare, who toddled downstairs, pushed in between her brother and her mother, held tightly round Hetty's legs and, on being told the news, jumped up and down shouting, 'Daddy, Daddy, Daddy, Daaaa-ddy!'

Then Hetty sprang into action, boiling the kettle, making tea, cutting bread, spreading jam, while talking through the news she had received and what she needed to do, what they needed to do.

'That was someone from a hospital not too far from here. It seems that your father did go across to Dunkirk, along with Roger Baldwin in his fishing boat. They rescued a dozen soldiers, but the boat sank less than two miles out from Dunkirk.'

'It wasn't seaworthy, Mum. Timothy Baldwin told me that.'

Hetty glanced sharply at Sam, then continued, 'It seems that most of the soldiers disappeared on to other boats, but one of them was badly wounded. Your father and another soldier kept him afloat between them while they held on to some wreckage. They were shot at by an enemy plane and your father was hit, but they were eventually rescued by the captain of a paddle steamer, which had also gone over to help with the evacuation of troops.'

'Where's Daddy now, Mummy? I want to see him, Mummy, I want to see him.'

Clare clambered down from the table, where she had been drinking her glass of milk, and pulled at Hetty's apron, as her mother put together a parcel of sandwiches and cakes and fruit.

'You'll see him very, very soon, poppet, but first he's got to have lots of rest.'

'But Dad's been gone nearly three weeks now, Mum. Why has it taken so long for anyone to tell us where he is?'

'It was a week before the paddle steamer made it back to England, by which time your father was very poorly. He kept slipping in and out of consciousness and was unable to tell anyone who he was. Apparently, he became delirious and thought he was in the trenches in the First World War. Anyway, what matters now is that he's on the mend and I must go and see him.'

'I'll do a picture for him, Mummy. He likes my pictures, doesn't he?'

Clare jumped down from the table again and ran up to her room.

'You'll tell him the pigeons are fine, won't you, Mum? Tell him he's got eight more youngsters waiting to meet their master.'

'Don't worry, Sam, I'll tell him what a brilliant job you're doing.'

Hetty set off to catch the next train, leaving Sam

to look after his sister, with the instruction that they were to go up the road to Mrs Humphreys if they had any problems. Clare was so excited that she dragged Sam off to see Mrs Humphreys anyway, and Sam was glad when Mrs Humphreys said he could have some time on his own.

He cleaned the pigeon-loft from top to bottom that morning. He emptied out the dirty straw, disinfected the floor, then covered it with a thick layer of fresh straw. He cleaned all the feeding troughs and water bottles. When he refilled the bowls in the nest-boxes, he was delighted to discover that four more eggs had hatched overnight. That brought the total to twelve since his father had been away, and left Sam with another four names to find. Two came to him straightaway – Colander and Dunkirk – though he had no idea what sex the squabs were. He scratched his head to come up with two more, and as he went back over the details of his father's escapade, he settled on Paddle and Steamer.

When he had finished with the pigeons, Sam began work on the vegetable plot. Although he and his mother had tried to keep the weeds down, their enthusiasm had waned in recent days, especially as fears for his father's safety had grown, and the garden had a certain air of neglect about it. He set to with a hoe and fork, leaving neat swathes of clear brown earth between each row of vegetables. Then he grabbed a bucket and went on slug and snail patrol, following their trails and picking dozens from the undersides of leaves, where they sheltered from the blistering sun while they feasted. Sam was ashamed to discover that it was too late for one row of lettuces. All that survived of them was a lattice-work of holes. He dug up the remains and sowed a new row of seeds, which he covered with a thin layer of soil and watered carefully.

For the first time in weeks, he felt happy. He hummed as he worked, and listened to the pigeons cooing reassuringly from the roof of their loft. It was going to be a good summer after all. If only Matt would come home, everything would be perfect.

For the next three weeks, Sam kept the garden and pigeon-loft in a permanent state of readiness for his father's return. Hetty visited Arthur every Wednesday and Saturday, leaving on the early morning train and arriving back late in the afternoon.

When she was away, Sam took Clare to and from school, and on Saturdays they spent at least part of the day at the Humphreys' farm, where Sam was allowed to ride on Mr Humphreys' tractor, while Clare collected eggs from the hens and helped Mrs Humphreys with her cooking.

Hetty returned from each visit with increasingly good news about their father's recovery. From being flat on his back and breathing with the aid of a venti-lator, he was able to sit up in bed and crack jokes with fellow patients. He was longing to be home, and missed Sam and Clare enormously.

'He's determined to be back for your birthday, Sam,' said Hetty.

'He'd better hurry up then, there's only two weeks to go.'

'He'll be there,' smiled Hetty, 'if I know your father. He won't want to miss out on your birthday cake.'

The following Saturday, Hetty was preparing to catch the early train as usual. Sam was still in bed, and Clare was playing with her dolls in her room.

Before she left, Hetty poked her nose round Sam's door and said, 'I've cut some bread ready for your breakfast and there's plenty of jam. Make sure Clare eats properly. Mrs Humphreys is going to feed you at lunchtime.' Hetty came over to the bed, bent over and touched Sam on the shoulder.

'We're nearly there, Sam,' she said quietly. 'I'm hoping your father will be able to come home later this week.'

Sam nodded sleepily.

'I don't know what I'd have done without you, Sam. You've kept me going, kept us all going.'

'Give Dad my love, Mum. Tell him I can't wait to see him.'

Hetty kissed Sam goodbye, and shortly after he heard the front door closing. He lay there dozing for a few minutes longer, before hearing footsteps cross his bedroom floor.

'Sammy – are you awake?'

Sam pretended to be asleep.

'I'm hungry, Sammy. Can we have breakfast?'

He felt Clare's soft breath stroke his cheek. He opened one eye, and closed it again quickly. Then he opened the other eye, and closed it. Clare began to giggle.

'I saw you winking at me, silly Samuel. Wake up, lazybones.'

Sam sat bolt upright in bed and said sternly, 'Did you call me lazybones, because if you did, I shall have to chase you.'

'Lazybones, lazybones, lazybones!' shrieked Clare. She leapt away from the bed and scampered out of the room, laughing hysterically. Sam threw back his covers and stomped after her, growling gruesomely, 'I'm a big monster from outer space and I'm coming to get you!'

'You can't catch me, you big old monster you!' shouted Clare, slipping past his outstretched arms and running downstairs.

'Oh yes I can,' growled Sam, gallumphing after her.

'Oh no you can't!'

Clare ran to the back door and unlocked it and Sam came into the kitchen. Just as Clare opened the door an overwhelming high-pitched whine filled the room.

'What's that noise, Sammy? I don't like it,' wailed Clare, putting her fingers in her ears and pushing the door to.

For a moment, Sam stood rooted to the spot. Something wrenched at his subconscious. Then he grabbed Clare and pulled her under the kitchen table. Seconds later, a loud explosion shook the house and blew the windows in. Clare screamed as glass sprayed across the room and showered the floor. Sam held her as tightly as he could, her head against his chest, his head on top of hers. They sat for minutes, locked in each other's arms, Clare sobbing and asking for her mother, Sam wondering where the bomb had fallen, for he was sure that's what it was, and whether there would be more. At last, he said, 'I'm just going to look out of the window.'

'Don't leave me, Sammy, don't leave me,' screamed Clare.

'I'll be one second, I'll come straight back.'

'I want to come too, Sammy, don't leave me.'

'No, Clare. Do as you're told. Stay there until I say so.'

Sam regretted shouting, but at least his sister stayed put. He slid out from under the table and picked his way over the glass towards the window.

What he saw when he looked out numbed him with shock. Where Arthur's vegetable garden had been, there was nothing but a huge crater.

'What is it, Sammy? I want to see.'

Sam stood confounded by the momentousness of what had happened.

'I want to see, Sammy, let me see.'

Clare was crawling out from under the table. The crunch of glass alerted Sam. He was about to stop her, but just then there was an urgent knocking at the front door. In a wild moment, Sam thought it might be the Germans, and fear shot through him like a bolt. Roughly he pushed Clare back under the table and ducked down himself. More knocking, then the door opened and a woman's voice called,

'Samuel? Clare? Are you all right?'

'Mrs Humphreys!' cried Clare. 'It's Mrs Humphreys!'

A wave of relief washed over Sam as his sister pushed him out of the way, scrambled to her feet and threw herself into Mrs Humphreys' generous bosom. Mr Humphreys stood just behind her and surveyed the room.

'There was a great big noise, Mrs Humphreys, and the windows smashed to pieces and I didn't like it and we hid under the table.'

'I know, my poppet, but are you both all right?'

'I cut my finger.'

Clare held up her finger with its tiny droplet of blood for Mrs Humphreys to inspect.

'You'll be needing a sweetie to make that better,' Mrs Humphreys declared solemnly.

Clare nodded and stuck her thumb in her mouth. Mr Humphreys looked concernedly at Sam.

'Are you all right, Sam?'

'There's not much left of the garden,' Sam said quietly.

'Thank goodness it missed the house. You were very lucky.'

The pigeons! What about the pigeons?

'I'll go and fetch the authorities. I'm pretty sure that was probably a leftover from a raid somewhere else. There was only one plane. The pilot must have dumped the rest of his load before going home. Don't go outside though, lad, will you? It might be dangerous.'

Sam nodded to Mr Humphreys as he left. What about the pigeons though? Did it miss the pigeons?

'You'll have to come and stay at the farm with us until your mummy comes back.' Mrs Humphreys was keen to get away.

'Can I play with Roly?' Clare asked instantly, tugging at Mrs Humphreys' elbow.

Please tell me the pigeons are all right.

'I'm sure he'd love you to. He didn't like that big noise either. What about you, Sam?'

'I'll clear up a bit and let the police in, then I'll come,' said Sam, determined not to leave before he was ready.

'Well, if you're sure,' said Mrs Humphreys doubtfully. 'Don't go outside though, eh, lad, just in case ... Mr Humphreys will be back soon, anyway.'

Sam gave a brief nod, and watched his sister trail uncertainly down the path and along the road, thumb in mouth, holding on tightly to Mrs Humphreys' hand, looking back every few yards.

As soon as they were out of sight, he closed the front door and walked slowly towards the kitchen window. He gazed again at the sunken garden, and then beyond to where his father's loft had stood for the past twenty years, ever since Arthur had first been introduced to pigeons to help him forget the horrors of the First World War.

The front of the loft and its roof had been blown away. The nest-boxes were hanging in tattered shards, but the perches were curiously untouched, and stuck out defiantly from the back wall. One of the pigeons was dangling lifelessly above the remains of its nest-box, pinned to the wall like a collector's trophy by a piece of wood which had speared its wing. Another, Sam could see, was hanging by its head from a delirious tangle of wire mesh. Sam turned away briefly, it was too much to bear, then cast his eyes straight back to the devastation that was his father's passion.

Not all of them? Surely not all of them?

Nothing moved. Nothing. The sky stayed blue and cloud-free, the sun shone, but the stillness was terrifying.

Sam opened the back door and went out. The air

was thick with dust, and the blistering heat engulfed him as he skirted his way carefully round the left side of the crater, which was overhung by the shredded remnants of his father's runner beans. A pigeon lay on its back by the fence, apparently unharmed, but its bright orange eyes were unseeing, and who knew what damage its shimmering feathers shrouded. 'Hotspur,' Sam whispered. One of Arthur's oldest males. Another sat in a bush, just as though that was where it had chosen to perch, except that its feet were gripping gaps in between the branches and its head was flopped to one side at a grotesque and impossible angle. 'Pipkin,' Sam whispered. Only a year old, but great potential his father had told him.

Sam reached the end of the garden and walked along the broken path towards the loft. Heaps of splintered wood and straw were strewn across the ground, forming a makeshift graveyard for the unrecognisable corpses that were littered amongst them. The floor of the loft held the greatest carnage. The straw that Sam had changed only that morning was matted with bloody feathers and shattered bodies which, in the stultefying heat, were already attracting flies.

Not all of them. Surely not all of them?

Sam wiped the perspiration from his forehead and scanned the hideous mess for some sign of life. Then he turned towards the house and looked up at the roof. Some of the pigeons sunbathed there when the roof of the loft was too crowded. They would have survived, wouldn't they? But, even if they had, the blast would certainly have frightened them away, perhaps for ever. And then, as Sam turned round again, he found hope. Sticking up through the straw, a wing moved, the slightest whimper of a move, but a move nonetheless. Sam bent down and carefully cleared the straw away. Beneath it, a soft, warm body sighed. Sam knelt down, cupped his hands and gently lifted the pigeon free. 'Mellow Yellow,' he whispered. The pigeon's pale yellow eyes were half closed as though the effort to open them wide was just too great. Sam leant over her to shield her from the dazzle of the sun and willed her to fight for her life. Close by, one of the pigeons' water bottles lay miraculously intact. He picked it up and encouraged his patient to drink, and she opened her beak a fraction but not enough. Every so often she shifted her weight slightly and fidgeted a foot, but then she became quiet again. Soon, her head drooped, her eyes closed, and her tiny heart stopped beating.

Sam sat back on his heels and tears rolled down his face. He laid Mellow Yellow's body on the ground and covered it with straw. 'I tried, Dad,' he wept. 'I really tried.' Then anger began to well up inside him and he couldn't stop it, didn't want to stop it. He stood up and shouted, 'Why? Why?'

The lack of any answer made him angrier still. He grabbed the water bottle and hurled it across the garden, watched it hit the fence and smash into pieces. 'Why?' he sobbed.

A loud hammering on the front door brought Sam back to his senses. Help had arrived. He no longer had to shoulder this burden on his own. Here were people who could deal with the worst of disasters. But Sam knew in an instant that he didn't want their help. He wanted to cope with this himself. He had managed so far. He didn't want people fussing around him, asking if he was all right, pushing him into a role of victim, invalid, child. He knew, too, that there was nothing he could do to prevent it. They would steamroller over him in their righteous determination to take control.

'Are you all right, lad?'

A police sergeant stood at the back door, a gaggle of heads craning their necks behind him. Sam nodded.

'Bit of a mess, eh?'

Sam watched as the group of men pushed into the garden and stared in disbelief. Among them Sam recognised the Air Raid Precautions warden, who smiled at him sympathetically, Roger Baldwin, who avoided looking him in the eye, and Mr Humphreys. They began to tread warily round the crater, scrutinising its depths as though expecting to see some sign of the alien form that had caused such damage. Then they stopped by the back wall of the pigeon loft and talked in lowered voices. Roger Baldwin fingered the trophy pigeon, and Sam wanted to yell at him to leave it alone.

'Where's your mother?' the police sergeant asked.

'She's gone to visit my father in hospital.'

Mr Humphreys came over to save Sam from further explanations.

'Arthur was badly injured helping with the Dunkirk rescue. He's been convalescing and is due back in a few days.'

'Not much of a homecoming for him,' the police sergeant observed. 'Well, we'd better find someone to look after you until your mother comes home. Meanwhile, we'll do our best to clear up here.'

'I don't need someone to look after me,' Sam protested. 'I'm all right.'

'I wouldn't be doing my duty, lad, if I didn't make sure you were looked after properly. It's not every day you have a bomb drop in your garden.'

Mr Humphreys smiled encouragingly at Sam. 'Don't worry, Sergeant, I'll stay with the lad, while these chaps here fetch some equipment to clear up the mess. It's his home, after all, and I'm sure his mother will want him to be here when she gets back.'

Sam was grateful again to Mr Humphreys.

'Right, then,' said the sergeant, suddenly brisk and ready to move on to his next assignment. 'Let's just hope that's the one and only time we see a hole in the ground round here.'

The men filed out of the house, some of them offering commiserations to Sam, others patting his back to tell him what a lucky boy he was. Sam sat down on the back doorstep, while Mr Humphreys picked up a broom and began to sweep up the glass on the kitchen floor.

'Close shave, eh, lad?'

'Not for Dad's pigeons. What's he going to say when he comes home?'

'He'll just be glad you and the rest of the family are safe, I reckon.'

'But he's spent years building up his loft, and now look at it.'

Sam stared across the garden and couldn't help feeling that, although he had tried so hard, he had somehow failed his father.

'All right, it'll be a big blow to him,' Mr Humphreys agreed, 'but he's suffered worse and come back fighting, and he'll do it again if I know anything about anything. There's a war on, lad, and war is a messy business. No one comes away from it unscathed.'

A sudden gentle whirring of wings made Sam look up. Above the shattered loft, a pigeon was gliding, dipping uncertainly, then rising again. Sam's heart skipped a beat. He stood up and, squinting in the bright sunlight, tried to see it properly as it hovered above the garden. Behind him, Mr Humphreys stopped sweeping and came to the door. The sudden movement made the bird fly off.

'That one of yours?' he asked.

Sam didn't answer. He walked slowly, quietly, to the hedge at the side of the garden, and stared across the field to where the pigeon had alighted on the roof of one of the barns.

'Come here, boy,' he whispered. 'Come here and let me see you.' Then he turned to Mr Humphreys and said, 'Keep very still or you'll frighten him away.'

Minutes later, the pigeon took off from the barn, flew over the loft again, and landed on the roof of the house.

'It's the Duke of Wellington!' Sam could scarcely contain his excitement. 'I'm sure it's the Duke of Wellington. He's not supposed to be here.'

'And where is he supposed to be?' Mr Humphreys smiled.

'He's working for the Intelligence Services. He should be flying back to their loft.'

Sam screwed up his eyes and stared at the pigeon again. 'He's carrying a message, look, round his leg!'

'Well I never!' exclaimed Mr Humphreys.

'I'll have to catch him. Don't make a noise, Mr Humphreys, and watch where he goes if he flies off.'

Catching the Duke of Wellington wasn't going to be easy. With the loft blown to pieces, the safe roosting place he remembered had gone. Sam could only hope that the lure of food would bring him down from the roof, but his father's supplies had disappeared along with the garden shed. He went indoors to delve into his mother's cupboards for something suitable, and came up with some peas, breadcrumbs and leftover rice. He found one of his father's pigeon baskets in the cupboard-under-the-stairs, and went quietly back outside.

'Poor fellow looks exhausted,' observed Mr Humphreys.

'I'm hoping he's hungry,' said Sam.

He laid a small trail of rice along the ground and positioned the basket on its side at the end of the trail. He placed a bowl of food inside the basket, then tied on a piece of string which he could pull to shut the lid as soon as the pigeon had entered. Finally, he stood a little way away from the basket and whistled encouragement, just as he had heard his father do.

At first, the Duke of Wellington looked at Sam but made no effort to move. Five minutes went by, with Sam whistling intermittently and the bird cocking its head as if to listen more carefully. Then, it stood and sidestepped uncertainly along the edge of the gutter.

'Come on, boy, come on,' Sam urged.

Another few minutes passed. The pigeon tottered backwards and forwards along the gutter, gazing intently at the trail of food, opening its wings every so often, then closing them again. At last, it launched itself in the air, hovered for a moment burbling softly, then dropped down on to the ground and began to feed. In no time, it had eaten its way to the end of the trail and was peering curiously into the basket. With scarcely any hesitation, it stepped inside, and Sam was able to close the lid.

'Well done, Sam. Your father would be proud of you.' Mr Humphreys patted him on the shoulder. 'Now, we'd better take that message to the police. They won't be too happy if we open it ourselves.'

'I'll go,' Sam said immediately. This was his show, he wasn't going to allow someone else to take over.

'Yes, you go,' grinned Mr Humphreys. 'One trip to the local constabulary is enough for me for one day. I'll just pop home to let Mrs Humphreys know what's happening, then I'll come back to help with the clearing up.'

Sam fastened the basket securely to the back of his bike. He was about to set off when he turned to Mr Humphreys and said, 'Mr Humphreys, please will you tell Clare that the Duke of Wellington has come home? I think she'd like to know.'

'Of course, lad. Now go carefully.'

# CHAPTER TWENTY

Sam pedalled as fast as he could along the road towards the village. He was on a mission of great importance. The message attached to the Duke of Wellington's leg might be a matter of life and death, and it was up to him, Samuel Lonsdale, to make sure it was delivered with the utmost speed. Let no man nor beast stand in my way!

By the time he reached the police house, he was sweating profusely and out of breath. He leaned his bike against the wall of the building, and panicked briefly that it might be recognised as one of the ones that had been 'stolen' a few weeks earlier. He dismissed the thought, for there was nothing particularly distinctive about his bike, and began to unstrap the pigeon basket. He was aware then of someone hovering behind him. Was he about to feel the hand of the law on his shoulder? He turned nervously, and came face to face with Timothy Baldwin.

'What's in the basket?' the boy asked, trying not to sound as though he cared.

'One of my father's pigeons,' Sam replied.

'Let's see then.' It was more of a demand than a request.

'I'm in a hurry,' Sam said dismissively. 'He's carrying a message and I've got to tell the police. It might be very important.'

'What sort of a message?'

Sam felt himself growing angry. 'Look, you don't really give a damn, so just go away.'

'I was only asking.'

Sam looked at the boy's bemused face, picked up the basket and went inside.

When he came back outside, flushed with pleasure at the praise and thanks he had received, Timothy Baldwin was waiting for him.

'You still got the bird then?' he said, pointing to the basket.

'Of course,' said Sam. 'The police wouldn't know

what to do with him. They just took the message from his leg.'

'Can I see him now, then?'

Sam eyed the boy suspiciously. What was he up to? Still, no harm could come right in front of the police house. He opened the basket just enough for Timothy to be able to peer inside. The Duke of Wellington cooed and burbled and blinked at the influx of light.

'What's his name?' Timothy Baldwin asked.

'The Duke of Wellington,' Sam answered hesitantly. But although the boy laughed out loud, it wasn't spiteful, in fact it was more in appreciation of such preposterousness.

Sam strapped the basket to the back of his bicycle, then, as he straddled the saddle and put his feet on the pedals, he heard his old enemy saying, very quietly, 'It's good news that your dad's going to be home soon', before turning on his heel and marching off down the road, hands thrust deep into his pockets.

'It's good news that your dad's going to be home soon.' Sam replayed the words over and over in his mind as he cycled slowly along the country lanes. 'It's good news that your dad's going to be home soon,' he called out to the Duke of Wellington. 'That was as close to an apology as I'm going to get, I think.'

He stopped to rest by the gate of a field. 'The battle is over, I am accepting a truce,' he tried out, and liked the way it sounded. He addressed the Duke of Wellington again: 'It's time for a fresh start, old man, and you'll have to be part of it, because you're staying with us no matter what Dad says.'

It was late afternoon by the time Sam reached the last bend before the home stretch of his journey. He was becoming apprehensive about seeing again the devastation of all that his father had achieved, when he rounded the corner and there, a few hundred yards ahead of him, he caught sight of a familiar but not so familiar figure tramping along. The hair was long and wild, the shoulders badly hunched under the weight of a backpack, the long coat and heavy boots caked in mud, but the gait was unmistakable. 'Matt?' Sam hardly dared say his name. 'Matt?' Then, when there was no possibility he could be wrong, he shrieked 'Matt!' at the top of his voice, jumped off his bike, laid it against a wall, and ran like a madman towards him. As soon as he felt his brother's arms close round him, he found himself crying and laughing and hugging and so full of joy that he couldn't speak.

'This is a nice welcome,' Matt said lightly, and then he said it again, but this time he held Sam so tight and his breathing was so laboured that Sam knew his brother was struggling not to break down. For several long seconds, they stood locked together in their shared need, until Matt suddenly said,

'Let me look at you then.' He held Sam at arm's length and studied him appraisingly. 'Goodness, how you've grown!' he exclaimed deliberately, and they both fell about laughing because it's what grown-ups always say to children when they haven't seen them for a while.

'Goodness, how you pong!' Sam managed to squeeze out when he had recovered some breath, and promptly broke into more hoots of laughter.

'How are the midges then, little brother, since we seem to have strayed into that sort of subject area?'

'Gone,' said Sam triumphantly, 'all gone.'

'That's what I want to hear,' said Matt. 'And Mum, and Dad, and Clare?'

Sam hesitated, then replied, 'They're fine, they're all fine, but a lot's happened since you've been away, Matt.'

'Yes,' Matt said quietly. 'A lot has happened, but as long as the five of us are all right … Come on, take me home now, Sam, I've only got two weeks till I go back, so I want to make the most of it. You can tell me what I've missed on the way.'

Sam went to pick up his bicycle and caught up again with his brother.

'You don't mind if the Duke of Wellington joins us, do you? I've become rather attached to him.' Sam grinned sheepishly.

'Ha, ha!' teased Matt. 'Bitten by the bug, are you?'

'No,' Sam denied hotly. 'You and your midges and bugs. We've just come to a sort of understanding, that's all.'